'You act as if I'm your wife!'

One eyebrow rose in cynical query. 'My dear Alyse, I have in my possession a marriage certificate stating clearly that you are.'

'You know very well what I mean!'

'Does it bother you that I accord you a measure of husbandly affection?'

'Courteous attention I can accept,' she acknowledged angrily. 'But intimate contact is totally unnecessary.'

His smile was peculiarly lacking in humour. 'I haven't even begun with intimacy.'

THE STEFANOS MARRIAGE

BY
HELEN BIANCHIN

MILLS & BOON LIMITED
ETON HOUSE   18-24 PARADISE ROAD
RICHMOND   SURREY   TW9 1SR

First published in Great Britain 1990 by Mills & Boon Limited

© Helen Bianchin 1990

Australian copyright 1990 Philippine copyright 1990 This edition 1991

ISBN 0 263 76914 3

Set in Times Roman 11 on 11½ pt. 01-9101-48320 C

Made and printed in Great Britain

CHAPTER ONE

THE traffic was unusually heavy as Alyse eased her stylish Honda hatchback on to the Stirling highway. From this distance the many tall buildings etched against the city skyline appeared wreathed in a shimmering haze, and the sun's piercing rays reflected against the sapphire depths of the Swan River as she followed its gentle curve into the heart of Perth.

Parking took an age, and she uttered a silent prayer in celestial thanks that she wasn't a regular city commuter as she competed with the early-morning populace striding the pavements to their individual places of work.

A telephone call from her solicitor late the previous afternoon requesting her presence in his office as soon as possible was perplexing, to say the least, and a slight frown creased her brow as she entered the modern edifice of gleaming black marble and non-reflecting tinted glass that housed his professional suite.

Gaining the foyer, Alyse stepped briskly towards a cluster of people waiting for any one of three lifts to transport them to their designated floor. As she drew close her attention was caught by a tall, dark-suited man standing slightly apart from the rest, and her eyes lingered with brief curiosity.

Broad-chiselled facial bone-structure in profile provided an excellent foil for the patrician slope of his nose and rugged sculptured jaw. Well-groomed thick dark hair was professionally shaped and worn fractionally longer than the current trend.

In his mid-thirties, she judged, aware there was something about his stance that portrayed an animalistic sense of power—a physical magnetism that was riveting.

As if he sensed her scrutiny, he turned slightly, and she was shaken by the intensity of piercing eyes that were neither blue nor grey but a curious mixture of both.

Suddenly she became supremely conscious of her projected image, aware that the fashionably tailored black suit worn with a demurely styled white silk blouse lent a professional air to her petite frame and shoulder-length strawberry-blonde hair, which, combined with delicate-boned features, reflected poise and dignity.

It took every ounce of control not to blink or lower her eyes beneath his slow analytical appraisal, and for some inexplicable reason she felt each separate nerve-ending tense as a primitive emotion stirred deep within her, alien and unguarded.

For a few timeless seconds her eyes seemed locked with his, and she could have sworn the quickening beat of her heart must sound loud enough for anyone standing close by to hear. A reaction, she decided shakily, that was related to nothing more than recognition of a devastatingly sexual alchemy.

No *one* man deserved to have such power at his command. Yet there was a lurking cynicism, a slight wariness apparent beneath the sophisticated veneer, almost as if he expected her to instigate an attempt at conversation, initiating a subtle invitation—to God knew what? Her *bed*?

Innate pride tinged with defiance lent her eyes a fiery sparkle and provided an infinitesimal tilt to her chin as she checked the hands of the clock positioned high on the marble-slabbed wall.

Two lifts reached the ground floor simultaneously, and she stood back, opting to enter the one closest her, aware too late that the man seemed intent on following in her wake.

The lift filled rapidly, and she determinedly fixed her attention on the instrument panel, all too aware of the man standing within touching distance. Despite her four-inch stiletto heels he towered head and shoulders above her, and this close she could sense the slight aroma of his cologne.

It was crazy to feel so positively *stifled*, yet she was supremely conscious of every single breath, every pulsebeat. It wasn't a sensation she enjoyed, and she was intensely relieved when the lift slid to a halt at her chosen floor.

Alyse's gratitude at being freed from his unsettling presence was short-lived when she discovered that he too had vacated the lift and was seemingly intent on entering the same suite of offices.

Moving towards Reception, she gave her name and that of the legal partner with whom she had an appointment, then selected a nearby chair. Reaching for a magazine, she flipped idly through the glossy pages with pretended interest, increasingly aware of the man standing negligently at ease on the edge of her peripheral vision.

With a hand thrust into the trouser pocket of his impeccably tailored suit he looked every inch the powerful potentate, portraying a dramatic mesh of blatant masculinity and elemental ruthlessness. Someone it would be infinitely wiser to have as a friend than an enemy, Alyse perceived wryly.

Something about him bothered her—an intrinsic familiarity she was unable to pinpoint. She knew they had never met, for he wasn't a man you would forget in a hurry!

'Miss Anderson? If you'd care to follow me, Mr Mannering will see you now.'

Alyse followed the elegantly attired secretary down a wide, spacious corridor into a modern office offering a magnificent view of the city. Acknowledging the solicitor's greeting, she selected one of three armchairs opposite his desk and graciously sank into its leather-cushioned depth.

'There seems to be some urgency in your need to see me,' she declared, taking time to cross one slim nylon-clad leg over the other as she looked askance at the faintly harassed-looking man viewing her with a degree of thoughtful speculation.

'Indeed. A most unexpected development,' Hugh Mannering conceded as he reached for a manilla folder and riffled through its contents. 'These papers were delivered by courier yesterday afternoon, and followed an hour later by a telephone call from the man who instigated their dispatch.'

A slight frown momentarily creased her brow. 'I thought Antonia's estate was quite straightforward.'

'Her estate—yes. Custody of your sister's son, however, is not.'

Alyse felt something squeeze painfully in the region of her heart. 'What do you mean?'

He bent his head, and his spectacles slid fractionally down his nose, allowing him the opportunity to view her over the top of the frame. 'I have copies of legal documentation by a delegate of the Stefanos family laying claim to Georg——' he paused to consult the name outlined within the documented text '——Georgiou. Infant son of Georgiou Stavro Stefanos, born to Antonia Grace Anderson at a disclosed maternity hospital in suburban Perth just over two months ago.'

Alyse paled with shock, her eyes large liquid pools mirroring disbelief as she looked at the solicitor with mounting horror. 'They can't do that!' she protested in a voice that betrayed shaky incredulity.

The man opposite appeared nonplussed. 'Antonia died intestate, without written authority delegating legal responsibility for her son. As her only surviving relative, you naturally assumed the role of surrogate mother and guardian.' He paused to clear his throat. 'However, technically, the child is an orphan, and a decision would, in the normal course of events, be made by the Department of Family Services as to the manner in which the child is to be cared for, having regard to all relevant circumstances with the welfare of the child as the paramount consideration. An application to adopt the child can be lodged with the Department by any interested party.' He paused to spare her a compassionate glance. 'A matter I had every intention of bringing to your attention.'

'Are you trying to say that my sister's lover's family have as much right to adopt her son as I do?' Alyse demanded in a fervent need to reduce reiterated legalese to its simplest form.

The solicitor's expression mirrored his spoken response. 'Yes.'

'But that's impossible! The clear facts of Georgiou's chosen dissociation from Antonia's letters would be a mark against him in any court of law.'

Tears welled unbidden as Alyse thought of her sister. Six years Alyse's junior, Antonia had been so carefree, so *young*. Too young at nineteen to suffer the consequences of a brief holiday romance abroad. Yet suffer she did, discovering within weeks of her return from an idyllic cruise of the Greek Islands that her capricious behaviour had resulted in pregnancy.

A letter dispatched at once to an address in Athens brought no response, nor, several weeks later, with the aid of a translator, did attempted telephone contact, for all that could be determined was that the number they sought was ex-directory and therefore unobtainable.

Truly a love-child, little Georgiou had survived by his mother's refusal to consider abortion, and he'd entered the world after a long struggle that had had the medics in attendance opting for surgical intervention via emergency Caesarian section. Fate, however, had delivered an incredibly cruel blow when complications which had plagued Antonia since giving birth had brought on a sudden collapse, followed within days by her tragic death.

Shattered beyond belief, Alyse had stoically attended to all the relevant arrangements, and employed a manageress for her childrenswear boutique during those first terrible weeks until she could arrange for a reliable babysitter.

Now, she had organised a satisfactory routine whereby a babysitter came in each morning, and the boutique was managed during the afternoon hours, thus ensuring that Alyse could spend as much time as possible with a young baby whose imposing Christian name had long since been affectionately shortened to Georg.

'I can understand your concern, Alyse. Mr Stefanos has offered to explain, personally, the reasons supporting his claim.'

Undisguised surprise widened her eyes, followed immediately by a degree of incredible anger. 'He's actually *dared* to come here in person, after all this time?'

Hugh Mannering regarded her carefully for several seconds, then offered slowly, 'It's in your own interest to at least listen to what he has to say.'

The solicitor depressed a button on the intercom console and issued his secretary with appropriate instructions.

Within a matter of seconds the door opened, and the tall compelling-looking man who had succeeded in shattering Alyse's composure only half an hour earlier entered the room.

She felt her stomach lurch, then contract in inexplicable apprehension. Who *was* he? She had seen sufficient of Antonia's holiday snapshots to be certain that the reflection depicted on celluloid and *this* man were not one and the same.

Hugh Mannering made the introduction with polite civility. 'Alyse Anderson—Aleksi Stefanos.'

'Miss Anderson.' The acknowledgment was voiced in a deep, faintly accented drawl, and an icy chill feathered across the surface of her skin. His eyes swept her features in raking appraisal, then locked with her startled gaze for a brief second before he directed his attention to the man opposite.

'I presume you have informed Miss Anderson of the relevant details?'

'Perhaps Mr Stefanos,' Alyse stressed carefully as he folded his lengthy frame into an adjacent chair, 'would care to reveal precisely his connection with the father of my sister's child?'

There could be no doubt she intended war, and it irked her incredibly that he was amused beneath the thin veneer of politeness evident.

'Forgive me, Miss Anderson.' He inclined his head cynically. 'I am Georgiou's elder brother— stepbrother, to be exact.'

'One presumes Georg,' she paused, deliberately refusing to give the name its correct pronunciation, 'dispatched you as his emissary?'

The pale eyes hardened until they resembled obsidian grey shards. 'Georgiou is dead. A horrific car accident last year left him a paraplegic, and complications took their final toll little more than a month ago.'

Alyse's mind reeled at the implication of a bizarre coincidence as Aleksi Stefanos went on to reveal in a voice devoid of any emotion,

'My family had no knowledge of your sister's existence, let alone her predicament, until several carefully concealed letters were discovered a week after Georgiou's death. Time was needed to verify certain facts before suitable arrangements could be made.'

'What arrangements?'

'The child will, of course, be brought up a Stefanos.'

Alyse's eyes blazed with brilliant fire. 'He most certainly will not!'

'You contest my right to do so?'

'*Your* right?' she retorted deliberately.

'Indeed. As he is the first male Stefanos grandchild, there can be no question of his rightful heritage.'

'Georg's birth is registered as Georgiou *Anderson*, Mr Stefanos. And as Antonia's closest relative *I* have accepted sole responsibility for her son.'

He appeared to be visibly unmoved, and her chin lifted fractionally as she held his glittering gaze.

'Verification of blood groupings has established beyond doubt that my brother is the father of your sister's child,' he revealed with chilling cynicism.

Alyse felt the rush of anger as it consumed her slim frame. How dared he even *suggest* otherwise! 'What did you imagine Antonia had in mind when she dispatched those letters begging for help, Mr Stefanos?' she managed in icy rage. 'Blackmail?'

'The thought did occur.'

'Why,' she breathed with barely controlled fury, 'you insulting, arrogant——'

'Please continue,' he invited as she faltered to a speechless halt.

'Bastard!' she threw with disdain, and glimpsed an inflexible hardness in the depths of his eyes.

'Antonia had no need of *money*—your brother's, or that of his family. As Mr Mannering will confirm, both my sister and I benefited financially when our parents died some years ago—sufficient to ensure we could afford a comfortable lifestyle without the need to supplement it in any way other than with a weekly wage. On leaving school, Antonia joined me in business.' She had never felt so positively *enraged* in her life. 'Your brother, Mr Stefanos,' she stressed, 'proposed *marriage* during their shared holiday, and promised to send for Antonia within a week of his return to Athens for the express purpose of meeting his family and announcing their engagement.' Her eyes clouded with pain as she vividly recalled the effect Georgiou's subsequent rejection had had on her sister.

'Georgiou's accident occurred the day after his return,' Aleksi Stefanos told her. 'He lay in hospital unconscious for weeks, and afterwards it was some time before he became fully aware of the extent of his injuries. By then it was doubtful if he could foresee a future for himself in the role of husband.'

'He could have written!' Alyse exclaimed in impassioned condemnation. 'His silence caused Antonia months of untold anguish. And you underestimate my sister, Mr Stefanos,' she continued bleakly, 'if you think she would have rejected Georgiou simply because of his injuries. She loved him.'

'And *love*, in your opinion, conquers all?'

Her eyes gleamed with hidden anger, sheer prisms of deep blue sapphire. 'Antonia deserved the chance to prove it,' she said with quiet vehemence. Her chin lifted, tilting at a proud angle.

His raking scrutiny was daunting, but she refused to break his gaze. 'And you, Miss Anderson?' he queried with deceptive softness. 'Would *you* have given a man such unswerving loyalty?'

Alyse didn't deign to answer, and the silence inside the room was such that it was almost possible to hear the sound of human breathing.

'Perhaps an attempt could be made to resolve the situation?' Alyse heard the mild intervention and turned slowly towards the bespectacled man seated behind his desk. For a while she had forgotten his existence, and she watched as his glance shifted from her to the hateful Aleksi Stefanos. 'I know I can speak for Alyse in saying that she intends lodging an adoption application immediately.'

'Legally, as a single woman, Miss Anderson lacks sufficient standing to supersede my right to my brother's child,' Aleksi Stefanos declared with dangerous silkiness.

'Only if you're married,' Alyse insisted, directing the solicitor a brief enquiring glance and feeling triumphant on receiving his nod in silent acquiescence. 'Are you married, Mr Stefanos?'

'No,' he answered with smooth detachment. 'Something I intend remedying without delay.'

'Really? You're *engaged* to be married?' She couldn't remember being so positively *bitchy*!

'My intended marital status is unimportant, Miss Anderson, and none of your business.'

'Oh, but it is, Mr Stefanos,' she insisted sweetly. 'You see, if *marriage* is a prerequisite in my battle to adopt Georg, then I too shall fight you in the marriage stakes by taking a husband as soon as

possible.' She turned towards the solicitor. 'Would
that strengthen my case?'

Hugh Mannering looked distinctly uncomfort-
able. 'I should warn you against the folly of mar-
rying in haste, simply for the sole purpose of
providing your nephew with a surrogate father. Mr
Stefanos would undoubtedly contest the validity of
your motive.'

'As I would contest *his* motive,' she insisted
fiercely, 'if he were to marry immediately.'

'I'm almost inclined to venture that it's unfor-
tunate you could not marry each other,' Mr
Mannering opined, 'thus providing the child with
a stable relationship, instead of engaging in lengthy
proceedings with the Government's Family Services
Department to determine *who* should succeed as
legal adoptive parent.'

Alyse looked at him as if he had suddenly gone
mad. 'You can't possibly be serious?'

The solicitor effected an imperceptible shrug. 'A
marriage of convenience isn't an uncommon
occurrence.'

'Maybe not,' she responded with undue asperity.
'But I doubt if Mr Stefanos would be prepared to
compromise in such a manner.'

'Why so sure, Miss Anderson?' The drawled
query grated her raw nerves like steel razing through
silk.

'Oh, really,' Alyse dismissed, 'such a solution is
the height of foolishness, and totally out of the
question.'

'Indeed?' His smile made her feel like a dove
about to be caught up in the deadly claws of a ma-
rauding hawk. 'I consider it has a degree of merit.'

'While *I* can't think of anything worse than being imprisoned in marriage with a man like you!'

If he could have shaken her within an inch of her life, he would have done so. It was there in his eyes, the curious stillness of his features, and she controlled the desire to shiver, choosing instead to clasp her hands together in an instinctive protective gesture.

Against *what*? a tiny voice taunted. He couldn't possibly pose a threat, for heaven's sake!

'There's nothing further to be gained by continuing with this conversation.' With graceful fluidity she rose to her feet. 'Good afternoon, Mr Mannering,' she said with distinct politeness before spearing her adversary with a dark, venomous glance. '*Goodbye*, Mr Stefanos.'

Uncaring of the solicitor's attempt to defuse the situation, she walked to the door, opened it, then quietly closed it behind her before making her way to the outer office.

It wasn't until she was in her car and intent on negotiating busy traffic that reaction began to set in.

Damn. *Damn* Aleksi Stefanos! Her hands clenched on the wheel until the knuckles showed white, and she was so consumed with silent rage that it was nothing short of a miracle that she reached the boutique without suffering a minor accident.

CHAPTER TWO

THE remainder of the morning flew by as Alyse conferred with the boutique's manageress, Miriam Stanford, checked stock and tended to customers. It was almost midday before she was able to leave, and she felt immensely relieved to reach the comfortable sanctuary of her home.

As soon as the babysitter left, Alyse put a load of laundry into the washing machine, completed a few household chores, and was ready for Georg at the sound of his first wakening cry.

After changing him, she gave him his bottle, then made everything ready for his afternoon walk—an outing he appeared to adore, for he offered a contented smile as she placed him in the pram and secured the patterned quilt.

The air was fresh and cool, the winter sun fingering the spreading branches of trees lining the wide suburban street, and Alyse walked briskly, her eyes bright with love as she watched every gesture, every fleeting expression on her young nephew's face. He was so active, so alive for his tender age, and growing visibly with every passing day.

A slight frown furrowed her brow, and her features assumed a serious bleakness as she mentally reviewed the morning's consultation in Hugh Mannering's office. Was there really any possibility that she might fail in a bid to adopt Georg? *Could* the hateful Aleksi Stefanos's adoption application succeed? It was clear she must phone the solicitor as soon as possible.

On returning home Alyse gave Georg his bath, laughing ruefully as she finally managed to get his wriggling slippery body washed and dry, then dusted with talc and dressed in clean clothes. She gave him his bottle and settled him into his cot.

Now for the call to Hugh Mannering.

'Can I lose Georg?' Alyse queried with stark disregard for the conversational niceties.

'Any permanent resolution will take considerable time,' the solicitor stressed carefully. 'Technically, the Family Services Department investigates each applicant's capability to adequately care for the child, and ultimately a decision is made.'

'Off the record,' she persisted, 'who has the best chance?'

'It's impossible to ignore facts, Alyse. I've studied indisputable records documenting Aleksi Stefanos's financial status, and the man has an impressive list of assets.'

A chill finger slithered the length of her spine, and she suppressed the desire to shiver. 'Assets which far outstrip mine, I imagine?'

'My dear, you are fortunate to enjoy financial security of a kind that would be the envy of most young women your age. However, it is only a small percentage in comparison.'

'Damn him!' The oath fell from her lips in husky condemnation.

'The child's welfare is of prime importance,' the solicitor reminded her quietly. 'I'll have the application ready for your signature tomorrow.'

The inclination to have a snack instead of preparing herself a meal was all too tempting, and Alyse settled for an omelette with an accompanying salad, then followed it with fresh fruit.

She should make an effort to do some sewing— at least attempt to hand-finish a number of tiny smocked dresses which had been delivered to the house by one of her outworkers this morning. Certainly the boutique could do with the extra supplies.

The dishes done and the washing folded, Alyse collected a bundle of garments from its enveloping plastic and settled herself comfortably in the lounge with her sewing basket. Working diligently, she applied neat stitches with precise care, clipped thread, then deftly rethreaded the needle and began on the next garment.

Damn! The soft curse disrupted the stillness of the room. The third in an hour, and no less vicious simply because it was quietly voiced.

Alyse looked at the tiny prick of blood the latest needle stab had wrought, and raised her eyes heavenward in mute supplication.

Just this one garment, and she'd pack it all away for the evening, she pleaded in a silent deal with her favourite saint. Although it would prove less vexing if she cast aside hand-finishing for the evening and relaxed in front of the television with a reviving cup of coffee. Yet tonight she needed to immerse herself totally in her work in an attempt to alleviate the build-up of nervous tension.

Specialising in exquisitely embroidered babywear sold under her own label, *Alyse*, she had by dint of hard work, she reflected, changed a successful hobby into a thriving business. Now there was a boutique in a modern upmarket shopping centre catering for babies and young children's clothes featuring her own exclusive label among several imported lines.

Five minutes later Alyse breathed a sigh of relief as the tiny garment was completed. Stretching her arms high, she flexed her shoulders in a bid to ease the knot of muscular tension.

Georg's wakening cry sounded loud in the stillness of the house, and she quickly heated his bottle, fed him, then settled him down for the night.

In the hallway she momentarily caught sight of her mirrored reflection, and paused, aware that it was hardly surprising that the combination of grief and lack of appetite had reduced her petite form to positive slenderness. There were dark smudges beneath solemn blue eyes, and the angles of her facial bone-structure appeared delicate and more clearly defined.

Minutes later she sank into a chair in the lounge nursing a mug of hot coffee, longing not for the first time for someone in whom she could confide.

If her parents were still alive, it might be different, she brooded, but both had died within months of each other only a year after she had finished school, and she had been too busy establishing a niche in the workforce as well as guiding Antonia through a vulnerable puberty to enjoy too close an empathy with friends.

The sudden peal of the doorbell shattered the quietness of the room, and she hurried quickly to answer it, vaguely apprehensive yet partly curious as to who could possibly be calling at this time of the evening.

Checking that the safety chain was in place, she queried cautiously, 'Who is it?'

'Aleksi Stefanos.'

Stefanos. The name seemed etched in her brain with the clarity of diamond-engraved marble, and she closed her eyes in a purely reflex action as undisguised anger replaced initial shock.

'How did you get my address?' she wanted to know.

'The telephone directory.' His voice held an infinite degree of cynicism.

'How *dare* you come here?' Alyse demanded, trying her best to ignore the prickle of fear steadily creating havoc with her nervous system.

'Surely eight-thirty isn't unacceptably late?' his drawling voice enquired through the thick wood-panelled door, and she drew in a deep angry breath, then released it slowly.

'I have absolutely nothing to say to you.'

'May I remind you that I have every right to visit my nephew?'

For some inexplicable reason his dry mocking tones sent an icy chill feathering the length of her spine. *Damn* him! Who did he think he was, for heaven's sake?

'Georg is asleep, Mr Stefanos.'

Her curt dismissing revelation was greeted with ominous silence, and she unconsciously held her breath, willing him to go away.

'Asleep or awake, Miss Anderson, it makes little difference.'

Alyse closed her eyes and released her breath in one drawn-out sigh of frustration. Without doubt, Aleksi Stefanos possessed sufficient steel-willed de-

termination to be incredibly persistent. If she refused to let him see Georg tonight, he'd insist on
a suitable time tomorrow. Either way, he would
eventually succeed in his objective.

Without releasing the safety chain, she opened
the door a fraction, noticing idly that he had exchanged his formal suit for light grey trousers and
a sweater in fine dark wool. Even from within the
protection of her home, he presented a disturbing
factor she could only view with disfavour.

'Will you give me your word that you won't try
to abduct Georg?' she asked him.

His eyes flared, then became hard and implacable, his facial muscles reassembling over
sculptured bone to present a mask of silent anger.

'It isn't in my interests to resort to abduction,'
he warned inflexibly. 'Perhaps you should be reminded that your failure to co-operate will be taken
into consideration and assuredly used against you.'

The temptation to tell him precisely what he could
do with his legal advisers was almost impossible to
ignore, but common sense reared its logical head
just in time, and Alyse released the safety chain,
then stood back to permit him entry.

'Thank you.'

His cynicism was not lost on her, and it took
considerable effort to remain civil. 'Georg's room
is at the rear of the house.'

Without even glancing at him, she led the way,
aware that he followed close behind her. She didn't
consciously hurry, but her footsteps were quick, and
consequently she felt slightly breathless when she
reached the end of the hallway.

Carefully she opened the door, swinging it wide so the shaft of light illuminated the room. Large and airy, it had been converted to a nursery months before Georg's birth, the fresh white paint with its water-colour murals on each wall the perfect foil for various items of nursery furniture, and a number of colourful mobiles hung suspended from the ceiling.

Fiercely protective, Alyse glanced towards the man opposite for any sign that he might disturb her charge, and saw there was no visible change in his expression.

What had she expected? A softening of that hard exterior? Instead there was a curious bleakness, a sense of purpose that Alyse found distinctly chilling.

Almost as if Georg sensed he was the object of a silent battle, he stirred, moving his arms as he wriggled on to his back, his tiny legs kicking at the blanket until, with a faint murmur, he settled again.

Alyse wanted to cry out that Georg was *hers*, and nothing, *no one*, was going to take him away from her.

Perhaps some of her resolve showed in her expressive features, for she glimpsed a muscle tighten at the edge of Aleksi Stefanos's powerful jaw an instant before he moved back from the cot, and she followed him from the room, carefully closing the door behind her.

It appeared he was in no hurry to leave, for he entered the lounge without asking, and stood, a hand thrust into each trouser pocket.

'Perhaps we could talk?' he suggested, subjecting her to an analytical scrutiny which in no way enhanced her temper.

'I was under the impression we covered just about everything this morning.'

Chillingly bleak eyes riveted hers, trapping her in his gaze, and Alyse was prompted to comment, 'It's a pity Georgiou himself didn't accord his son's existence such reverent importance.'

'There were, I think you will have to agree, extenuating circumstances.'

'If he really did *love* my sister,' she stressed, 'he would have seen to it that someone—even *you*—answered any one of her letters. He had a responsibility which was ignored, no matter how bravely he grappled with his own disabilities.'

His gaze didn't waver. 'I imagine he was tortured by the thought of Antonia bearing a child he would never see.'

'The only bonus to come out of the entire débâcle is Georg.'

He looked at her hard and long before he finally spoke. 'You must understand, he cannot be raised other than as a Stefanos.'

Alyse saw the grim resolve apparent, and suddenly felt afraid. 'Why?' she queried baldly. 'A man without a wife could only offer the services of a nanny, which, even if it were a full-time live-in employment, can't compare with my love and attention.'

His shoulders shifted imperceptibly, almost as if he were reassembling a troublesome burden, and his features assumed an inscrutability she had no hope of penetrating.

'You too employ the part-time services of a nanny in the guise of babysitter. Is this not so?' An eyebrow slanted in silent query. 'By your own admission, you operate a successful business. With each subsequent month, my nephew will become more active, sleep less, and demand more attention. While you delegate, in part, your business duties, you will also be delegating the amount of time you can spend with Georg. I fail to see a significant difference between your brand of caring and mine.'

'On that presumption you imagine I'll concede defeat?' Alyse queried angrily.

'I would be prepared to settle an extremely large sum in your bank account for the privilege.'

She shook her head, unable to comprehend what she was hearing. 'Bribery, Mr Stefanos? No amount of money would persuade me to part with Antonia's son.' She cast him a look of such disdainful dislike, a lesser man would have withered beneath it. 'Now, will you please leave?'

'I haven't finished what I came to say.'

He must have a skin thicker than a rhinoceros! Alyse could feel the anger emanate through the pores of her skin until her whole body was consumed with it. 'If you don't leave *immediately*, I'll call the police!'

'Go ahead,' he directed with pitiless disregard.

'This is my home, dammit!' Alyse reiterated heatedly.

His eyes were dark and infinitely dangerous. 'You walked out on a legal consultation this morning, and now you refuse to discuss Georg's welfare.' It was his turn to subject her to a raking scrutiny, his smile wholly cynical as he glimpsed the tide of colour wash over her cheeks. 'I imagine the police will be sympathetic.'

'They'll also throw you out!'

'They'll suggest I leave,' he corrected. 'And conduct any further discussion with you via a legal representative.' He paused, and his eyes were hard and obdurate, reflecting inflexible masculine strength of will. 'My stepbrother's child has a legal right to his stake in the Stefanos heritage. It is what Georgiou would have wanted; what my father wants. If Antonia were still alive,' he paused deliberately, 'I believe *she* would have wanted her son to be acknowledged by her lover's family, and to receive the financial benefits and recognition that are his due.'

Alyse's eyes sharpened as their depths became clearly defined. 'I intend having you and your *family* fully investigated.'

As a possible threat, it failed dismally, for he merely acknowledged her words with a cynical smile.

'Allow me to give you the relevant information ahead of official confirmation.'

Beneath the edge of mockery was a degree of inimical anger that feathered fear down the length of her spine and raised all her fine body hairs in protective self-defence.

'My father and stepmother reside in Athens. *I*, however, left my native Greece at the relatively young age of twenty to settle in Australia. Initially Sydney—working as a builder's labourer seven days a week, contractual obligations and weather permitting. After three years I moved to the Gold

Coast, where I bought land and built houses before venturing into building construction. The ensuing thirteen years have escalated my company to a prestigious position within the building industry. Without doubt,' he continued drily, 'I possess sufficient independent wealth to garner instant approval with the Family Services Department, and there are no mythical skeletons in any one of my closets.'

'Hardly a complete résumé, Mr Stefanos,' Alyse discounted scathingly.

'How far back into the past do you wish to delve? Does the fact that my mother was Polish, hence my unusual Christian name, condemn me? That she died when I was very young? Is that sufficient, Miss Anderson?' One eyebrow slanted above dark eyes heavily opaque with the rigors of memory. 'Perhaps you'd like to hear that a sweet, gentle Englishwoman eased my father's pain, married him and bore a male child without displacing my position as the eldest Stefanos son or alienating my father's affection for me in any way. She became the mother I'd never known, and we keep in constant touch, exchanging visits at least once each year.'

'And now that Georgiou is dead, they want to play an integral part in Georg's life.' Alyse uttered the words in a curiously flat voice, and was unprepared for the whip-hard anger in *his*.

'Are you so impossibly selfish that you fail to understand what Georg's existence means to them?' he demanded.

'I know what it means to *me*,' she cried out, sorely tried. 'If Antonia hadn't written to Georgiou, if——'

'Don't colour facts with unfounded prejudice,' Aleksi Stefanos cut in harshly. 'The letters exist as irrefutable proof. *I* intend assuming the role of Georg's father,' he pursued, his voice assuming a deadly softness. 'Don't doubt it for a minute.'

'Whereas I insist on the role of *mother*!' she blazed.

'You're not prepared to compromise in any way?'

'*Compromise?* Are *you* prepared to compromise? Why should it be *me* who has to forgo the opportunity of happiness in a marriage of my choice?'

His eyes narrowed fractionally. 'Is there a contender waiting in the wings, Miss Anderson? Someone sufficiently foolish to think he can conquer your fiery spirit and win?'

'What makes you think *you* could?'

His eyes gleamed with latent humour, then dropped lazily to trace the full curve of her lips before slipping down to the swell of her breasts, assessing each feature with such diabolical ease that she found it impossible to still the faint flush of pink that coloured her cheeks.

'I possess sufficient experience with women to know you'd resent any form of male domination, yet conversely refuse to condone a spineless wimp who gave way to your every demand.' Alyse stood speechless as his gaze wandered back to meet hers and hold it with indolent amusement. A sensation not unlike excitement uncoiled deep within her, and spread throughout her body with the speed of liquid fire, turning all the highly sensitised nerve-endings into a state of sensual awareness so intense it made her feel exhilaratingly *alive*, yet at the same time terribly afraid.

'The man in my life most certainly won't be you, Mr Stefanos!' she snapped.

'One of the country's best legal brains has given me his assurance that my adoption application will succeed,' he revealed. 'This morning's consultation in Hugh Mannering's office was arranged because I felt honour-bound to personally present facts regarding my stepbrother's accident and subsequent death. As to Georg's future...' he paused significantly '...the only way you can have any part in it will be to opt for marriage—to me.'

'You alternately threaten, employ a form of emotional blackmail, attempt to buy me off, then offer a marriage convenient only to *you*?' The slow-boiling anger which had simmered long beneath the surface of her control finally bubbled over. 'Go to *hell*, Mr Stefanos!'

The atmosphere in the lounge was so highly charged, Alyse almost expected it to explode into combustible flame.

He looked at her for what seemed an age, then his voice sounded cold—as icy as an Arctic gale. 'Think carefully before you burn any figurative bridges,' he warned silkily.

Alyse glared at him balefully, hating him, abhorring what he represented. 'Get out of my house. *Now!*' Taut, incredibly angry words that bordered close on the edge of rage as she moved swiftly from the room.

In the foyer she reached for the catch securing the front door, then gasped out loud as Aleksi Stefanos caught hold of her shoulders and turned her towards him with galling ease.

One glance at those compelling features was sufficient to determine his intention, and she struggled fruitlessly against his sheer strength.

'The temptation to teach you the lesson I consider you deserve is almost irresistible,' he drawled.

His anger was clearly evident, and, hopelessly helpless, Alyse clenched her jaw tight as his head lowered in an attempt to avoid his mouth, only to cry out as he caught the soft inner tissue with his teeth, and she had no defence against the plundering force of a kiss so intense that the muscles of her throat, her jaw, screamed in silent agony as he completed a ravaging possession that violated her very soul.

Just as suddenly as it had begun, it was over, and she sank back against the wall, her eyes stricken with silent hatred.

At that precise moment a loud wailing cry erupted from the bedroom, and Alyse turned blindly towards the nursery. Crossing to Georg's cot, she leant forward and lifted his tiny body into her arms. He smelled of soap and talc, and his baby cheek was satin-smooth against her own as she cradled him close.

His cries subsided into muffled hiccups, bringing stupid tears to her own eyes, and she blinked rapidly to still their flow, aware within seconds that her efforts were in vain as they spilled and began trickling ignominiously down each cheek.

This morning life had been so simple. Yet within twelve hours Aleksi Stefanos had managed to turn it upside down.

She turned as the subject of her most dire thoughts followed her into the nursery.

'You bastard!' she berated him in a painful whisper. 'Have you no scruples?'

'None whatsoever where Georg is concerned,' Aleksi Stefanos drawled dispassionately.

'What you're suggesting amounts to emotional blackmail, damn you!' Her voice emerged as a vengeful undertone, and Georg gave a slight whimpering cry, then settled as she gently rocked his small body in her arms.

'What I'm suggesting,' Aleksi Stefanos declared hardily, 'is parents, a home, and a stable existence for Georg.'

'Where's the stability in two people who don't even *like* each other?' Damn him—who did he think he was, for heaven's sake?

An icy shiver shook her slim frame in the knowledge that he knew precisely who he was and the extent of his own power.

'The alternatives are specific,' he continued as if she hadn't spoken, 'the choice entirely your own. You have until tomorrow evening to give me your answer.'

She was dimly aware that he moved past her to open the door, and it was that final, almost silent click as he closed it behind him that made her frighteningly aware of his control.

CHAPTER THREE

ALYSE stood where she was for what seemed an age before settling Georg into his cot, then she moved slowly to the front of the house, secured the lock and made for her own room, where she undressed and slid wearily into bed.

Damn. *Damn* him, she cursed vengefully. Aleksi Stefanos had no right to place her in such an invidious position. For the first time she felt consumed with doubt, apprehensive to such a degree that it was impossible to relax.

Images flooded her mind, each one more painful than the last, and she closed her eyes tightly against the bitter knowledge that adoption was absolute, so *final*.

If Aleksi Stefanos was successful with his application, he would remove Georg several thousand kilometres away to the opposite side of the continent. To see him at all, she would have to rely on Aleksi Stefanos's generosity, and it would be difficult with her business interests, to be able to arrange a trip to Queensland's Gold Coast more than once a year.

The mere thought brought tears to her eyes, and she cursed afresh. At least divorced parents got to *share* custody of their children.

However, to become divorced, one first had to marry, Alyse mused in contemplative speculation. Maybe... No, it wasn't possible. Or was it? How

33

long would the marriage have to last? A year? Surely no longer than two, she decided, her mind racing.

If she did opt for marriage, she could have a contract drawn up giving Miriam a percentage of the profits, thus providing an incentive ensuring that the boutique continued to trade at a premium. As far as the house was concerned, she could lease it out. Her car would have to be sold, but that wouldn't matter, for she could easily buy another on her return.

A calculating gleam darkened her blue eyes, and a tiny smile curved her generous mouth.

When Aleksi Stefanos contacted her tomorrow, he would discover that she was surprisingly amenable. It was infinitely worth a year or two out of her life if it meant she got to keep Georg.

For the first time in the six weeks since Antonia's funeral, Alyse slept without a care to disturb her subconscious, and woke refreshed, eager to start the new day.

With so much to attend to, she drew up a list, and simply crossed every item off as she dealt with it.

A call to Hugh Mannering determined that marriage to Aleksi Stefanos would reduce the adoption proceedings to a mere formality, and he expressed delight that she was taking such a sensible step.

Alyse responded with a tongue-in-cheek agreement, and chose not to alarm her legal adviser by revealing the true extent of her plans.

Miriam was delighted to be promoted, and proved more than willing to assume management of the boutique for as long as necessary.

By late afternoon Alyse was able to relax, sure that everything was in place.

A light evening meal of cold chicken and salad provided an easy alternative to cooking, and she followed it with fresh fruit.

The telephone rang twice between seven and eight o'clock, and neither call was from Aleksi Stefanos.

A cloud of doubt dulled her eyes as she pondered the irony of him not ringing at all, only to start visibly when the insistent burr of the phone sounded shortly before nine.

It had to be him, and she let it peal five times in a fit of sheer perversity before picking up the receiver.

'Alyse?' His slightly accented drawl was unmistakable, his use of her Christian name an impossible liberty, she decided as she attempted to still a sense of foreboding. 'Have you reached a decision?'

He certainly didn't believe in wasting words! A tinge of anger heightened her mood. Careful, a tiny voice cautioned. You don't want to blow it. 'Yes.'

There was silence for a few seconds as he waited for her to continue, and when she didn't he queried with ill-concealed mockery, 'Must I draw it from you like blood from a stone?'

If it wasn't for Georg she'd slam down the receiver without the slightest compunction. 'I've considered your proposition,' she said tightly, 'and I've decided to accept.' There, she'd actually said it.

'My parents arrive from Athens at the beginning of next week,' Aleksi Stefanos told her without preamble, and she would have given anything to ruffle that imperturbable composure. 'They're naturally eager to see Georg, and there's no reason why you both shouldn't fly back to Queensland with me on Friday.'

'I can't possibly be ready by then,' Alyse protested, visibly shaken at the way he was assuming control.

'Professional packers will ensure that everything in the house is satisfactorily dealt with,' he said matter-of-factly. 'Whatever you need can be airfreighted to the Coast, and the rest put into storage. The house can be put into the hands of a competent letting agent, and managerial control arranged at the boutique. I suggest you instruct Hugh Mannering to draw up a power of attorney and liaise with him. All it takes is a few phone calls. To satisfy the Family Services Department, it would be advisable if a civil marriage ceremony is held here in Perth—Thursday, if it can be arranged. Relevant documentation regarding Georg's adoption can then be signed ready for lodgement, leaving us free of any added complications in removing him from the State.'

'Dear heaven,' Alyse breathed unsteadily, 'you don't believe in wasting time!'

'I'll give you a contact number where I can be reached,' he continued as if she hadn't spoken, relaying a set of digits she had to ask him to repeat as she quickly wrote them down. 'Any questions?'

'At least *ten*,' she declared with unaccustomed sarcasm.

'They can wait until dinner tomorrow evening.'

'With everything I have to do, I won't have *time* for dinner!'

'I'll collect you at six.'

There was a click as he replaced the receiver, and Alyse felt like screaming in vexation. What had she expected—small talk? *Revenge*, she decided, would be very sweet!

Removing the receiver, she placed a call to Miriam Stanford and asked if the manageress could work the entire day tomorrow, informed her briefly of her intended plans and promised she would be in at some stage during the afternoon.

Alyse slept badly, and rose just after dawn determined to complete a host of household chores, allowing herself no respite as she conducted a thorough spring-clean of the large old home, stoically forcing herself to sort through Antonia's possessions—something she'd continually put off until now.

It was incredibly sad, for there were so many things to remind her of the happy young girl Antonia had been, the affection and laughter they had shared. Impossible to really believe she was no longer alive, when celluloid prints and vivid memories provided such a painful reminder.

Despite her resolve to push Aleksi Stefanos to the edge of her mind, it was impossible not to feel mildly apprehensive as she settled Georg with the babysitter before retiring to the bathroom to shower, then dress for the evening ahead.

Selecting an elegant slim-fitting off-the-shoulder gown in deep sapphire blue, she teamed it with black stiletto-heeled shoes, tended to her make-up with painstaking care, then brushed her shoulder-length strawberry-blonde hair into its customary smooth bell before adding a generous touch of Van Cleef & Arpels' *Gem* to several pulsebeats. Her only added jewellery was a diamond pendant, matching earstuds and bracelet.

At five minutes to six she checked last-minute details with the babysitter, brushed a fleeting kiss to Georg's forehead, then moved towards the lounge, aware of a gnawing nervousness in the pit of her stomach with every step she took.

Now that she was faced with seeing him again, she began to wonder if she was slightly mad to toy with a man of Aleksi Stefanos's calibre. He undoubtedly ate little girls for breakfast, and although she was no naïve nineteen-year-old, her experience with men had been pitifully limited to platonic friendships that had affection as their base rather than any degree of passion. It hardly equipped her to act a required part.

Yet act she must—at least until she had his wedding ring on her finger. Afterwards she could set the rules by which the marriage would continue, and for how long.

Punctuality was obviously one of his more admirable traits, for just as she reached the foyer there was the soft sound of car tyres on the gravel drive followed almost immediately by the muted clunk of a car door closing.

At once she was conscious of an elevated nervous tension, and it took every ounce of courage to move forward and open the door.

Standing in its aperture, Aleksi Stefanos looked the epitome of male sophistication attired in a formal dark suit. Exuding more than his fair share of dynamic masculinity, he had an element of tensile steel beneath the polite veneer, a formidableness and sense of purpose that was daunting.

'Alyse.' There was an edge of mockery apparent, and she met his gaze with fearless disregard, blindly ignoring the increased tempo of her heartbeat.

Just a glance at the sensual curve of his mouth was enough to remember how it felt to be positively *absorbed* by the man, for no one in their wildest imagination could term what he had subjected her to as merely a *kiss*.

Conscious of his narrowed gaze, Alyse stood aside to allow him entry, acknowledging politely, 'Mr Stefanos.'

'Surely you can force yourself to say Aleksi?' he chastised with ill-concealed mockery.

Alyse choked back a swift refusal. Steady, she cautioned—anger will get you precisely nowhere. Opting for the line of least resistance, she ventured evenly, 'If you insist.' Remembering her manners, she indicated the lounge. 'Please come in. Would you care for a drink?'

'Unless you'd prefer one, I suggest we leave,' he countered smoothly. 'I've booked a table for six-thirty.'

Without a further word she preceded him to the car, allowing him to reach forward and open the door, and she slid into the passenger seat, aware of his close proximity seconds later as he slipped in behind the wheel and set the large vehicle in motion.

'Where are we dining?' As a conversational gambit, it was sadly lacking in originality, but anything was better than silence, Alyse decided wildly as they joined the flow of traffic leading into the city.

'My hotel.'

She turned towards him in thinly veiled aston-
ishment. 'I could have met you there.'

'Thus preserving feminine independence?' Aleksi
mocked as he spared her a quick assessing appraisal before returning his attention to the com-
puter-controlled intersection.

'I'll take a cab home.'

One eyebrow quirked in visible amusement as the
lights changed, and he eased the car forward. 'Impossible,' he declared smoothly, and she felt like
hitting him for appearing so damnably implacable.

'Would it dent your chauvinistic male ego?' she
queried sweetly, and heard his soft laughter.

'Not in the least. However, as my fiancée and
soon-to-be wife, you can't be permitted.'

She closed her eyes, then slowly opened them
seconds later. It was the only defence she had in
masking the incredible fury she harboured against
him.

As if he sensed her inner battle, he slid a tape
into the cassette-deck, and she leaned back against
the headrest, her eyes fixed on the tall city buildings
and the wide sweep of river.

Alyse was familiar with the hotel, if not the restaurant, and when they were seated she permitted
Aleksi to fill an elegant flute with Dom Perignon,
sipping the superb champagne in the hope that it
might afford her a measure of courage to face the
evening ahead.

Aleksi conferred with the waiter over the menu,
asking her what she wanted before placing their
order, then he leaned well back in his chair and
subjected her to a veiled scrutiny.

'Aren't you in the least curious to learn what arrangements I've made?'

She lifted her glass and took a generous swallow before replacing it on the table. 'I have no doubt you'll reveal them soon enough.' Tiny aerated bubbles of alcohol set up a tingling warmth inside her stomach and began transporting them through every vein in her body.

'We have an eleven o'clock appointment with the register office on Thursday, followed by a consultation with Hugh Mannering at two, and at three we're due to present ourselves at the Family Services Department. On Friday we catch the late morning flight en route to the Coast,' he informed her cynically.

The enormity of what she was about to undertake seemed to assume gigantic proportions, and she suffered his raking scrutiny with unblinking solemnity.

'This is no time for second thoughts,' Aleksi stated in a voice that was silky-smooth and infinitely dangerous. 'The reason for a marriage between us is obvious,' he declared hardily, 'and will be accepted as such.'

'Am I supposed to get down on my knees and kiss your feet in sheer gratitude for the privilege?' Her voice dripped ice, and she saw his blue-grey eyes assume a chilling ruthlessness.

'Careful,' he warned dangerously. 'I insist we present a veneer of politeness in the company of others.' He directed her a swift calculated appraisal that sent shivers of fear scudding the length of her spine. 'In private you can fight me as much as you like.'

'In private,' she conceded with ill-concealed fury, 'I shall probably render you grievous bodily harm!'

'Don't expect me not to retaliate,' he drawled.

'Do that, and I'll have you up for assault!'

His eyes narrowed and assumed the hue of a dark storm-tossed sea. 'I wasn't aware I alluded to physical abuse.'

Her eyes widened into huge pools of incredulity as comprehension dawned, and she fought valiantly against an all-encompassing anger. 'Abuse is still an ugly word, whether it be mental or physical,' she said tightly.

'Then perhaps you would be advised to keep a rein on your temper.'

'I must have been mad to agree to *any* alliance with you!' she declared bitterly, sure she'd become a victim of temporary insanity.

'Georg is the crux,' Aleksi remarked cynically, and she cried out in vengeful disavowal,

'I don't have much choice, damn you!'

'I offered you the opportunity of assuming the role of Georg's mother.'

'The only problem is that *you* form part of the package!'

'Oh, it mightn't be too bad.' His smile was totally lacking in humour. 'I live in a beautiful home—a showcase to display my expertise within the building industry. I enjoy the company of a close circle of friends, and frequently entertain. The Gold Coast is far from dull. I'm sure you'll manage to amuse yourself.'

'When do you intend informing your parents of our impending marriage?' asked Alyse.

'I already have,' he drawled with hateful cynicism. 'They're delighted that we've chosen such a sensible solution.'

'Are your parents visiting for very long?'

'Question-and-answer time, Alyse? Or simply sheer curiosity?'

An angry flush crept over her cheeks, and her eyes sparked with brilliant blue fire. 'I imagined it was a legitimate query.' If they'd been alone, she would have thrown the contents of her glass in his face. 'Perhaps I should opt for silence.'

'Apparent subservience?' he queried sardonically. 'Somehow I can't perceive you acquiring that particular mantle.'

'No,' Alyse agreed coolly out of deference to the waiter, who deftly removed their plates and busied himself serving the main course.

The grilled fish with hollandaise sauce and accompanying assortment of vegetables was assembled with artistic flair and infinitely tempting to the most discerning palate. Yet she was so incredibly angry she was hard pressed to do the course the justice it deserved. Afterwards she declined dessert and the cheeseboard, and simply opted for coffee, noting with silent rage that Aleksi Stefanos's appetite appeared totally unaffected.

'Perhaps you could bring yourself to tell me what progress *you* have made?' he suggested.

Alyse met his gaze with fearless disregard. 'Everything is taken care of—the boutique, leasing the house. All that remains for me to do is *pack*.'

'And shop for a wedding dress,' he added with hateful ease, one eyebrow slanting with a degree of mocking humour, and a diabolical imp prompted her to query,

'Traditional white?' Her own eyebrow matched his in a deliberate arch.

'Do you have any objection?'

You're darned right I have! she felt like screaming. 'Surely a civil ceremony doesn't warrant such extravagance?'

'Humour me.'

'The hell I will! A classic-designed suit is adequate.' She paused, her eyes wide and startlingly direct. 'In black, or red. Something that makes a definite statement.'

He leaned further back in his chair, his posture portraying indolent ease. Yet there was a degree of tightly coiled strength apparent, and a prickle of apprehension feathered the surface of her skin.

'Flamboyant reluctance?' Aleksi queried with deceptive mildness. 'You choose to be recorded for posterity in a manner that will doubtless raise questions from our son, ten—fifteen years from now?'

Her lips parted to say that ten years down the track she would no longer be his wife. In fact, the requisite two would be two too many! Except that no sound escaped as she snapped her mouth firmly closed. 'I'll agree to a cream linen suit, matching accessories and a floral bouquet,' she told him.

'Adequate,' he drawled. 'But not precisely what I had in mind.'

'Well, isn't that just too damned bad?' Alyse snapped with scant attempt at politeness. 'Perhaps you've decided to compound the farce with formal tails and an elegant striped silk cravat?'

'Are you usually so quarrelsome, or is your behaviour merely an attempt to oppose me?'

Her eyes flashed pure crystalline sapphire. 'Oh, both. I'm no timid little dove.'

A lazy smile broadened the generous curve of his mouth. 'Even the wildest bird can be trained to enjoy captivity.'

A surge of anger rose to the surface, bringing a tinge of pink to her cheeks and sharpening her features. 'That's precisely the type of sexist remark I'd expect you to make!' She looked at him with increasing hostility. 'If you've finished your coffee, I'd like to leave.'

'So early, Alyse?' he mocked as he signalled the waiter to bring their bill. 'You've no desire to go on to a nightclub?'

'What would be the point? We're at daggers drawn now!' She tempered the remark with a totally false smile that almost felled the waiter, but didn't fool Aleksi in the slightest.

'We'll doubtless shatter every romantic illusion your babysitter possesses if I return you before the witching hour of midnight,' he remarked.

'As there's nothing in the least romantic about our alliance, it hardly matters, does it?' She stood to her feet and preceded him from the restaurant, uncaring that he followed close behind.

In the car she sat in silence, conscious of the faint swish of tyres on the wet bitumen. There was movement everywhere, people walking, colourful flashes of neon as the large vehicle purred through the city streets, and she became fascinated by the reflection caught in the still waters of the Swan River as they headed west towards Peppermint Grove.

'I'll arrange for a chauffeured limousine to collect you at ten-thirty on Thursday morning,' Aleksi declared as he brought the car to a halt in her driveway. 'You have the phone number of my hotel if you need to contact me.'

Polite, distant, and totally businesslike. It was almost as if he was deliberately playing an extremely shrewd game with every single manoeuvre carefully planned, Alyse brooded, aware of a chill shiver that owed nothing to the cool midwinter temperature.

'I doubt if there'll be the necessity,' she declared as she reached for the door-clasp, only to catch her breath in startled surprise as he slid out from behind the wheel and walked round to open her door.

Moving swiftly from the passenger seat, she stood still, unsure of his intention, her movements momentarily suspended as she prepared for a rapid flight into the safety of the house. If he *dared* to kiss her, she'd hit him!

His faint mocking smile was almost her undoing, and she drew a deep steadying breath before issuing a stilted, 'Goodnight.'

Without so much as a backward glance she walked to the front door, put her key in the lock, then closed the door carefully behind her.

Inside was warmth and light, the endearing familiarity of a home where there were no shadows, no insecurity.

Summoning a smile as she moved into the lounge, she checked with the babysitter and paid her before looking in on Georg, then she simply locked up and prepared for bed.

CHAPTER FOUR

THE civil ceremony was incredibly brief, and only the fleeting appearance of Hugh Mannering provided a familiar face as Alyse affixed 'Stefanos' after 'Alyse' on the marriage certificate.

There were photographs, several of them taken by a professional, followed by lunch in the elegant dining-room of an inner city hotel.

Their appearance attracted circumspect interest. Her pencil-slim skirt with a long-line jacket in pale cream linen and matching accessories portrayed designer elegance, while Aleksi's impeccably tailored silver-grey suit merely accentuated his magnetic masculine appeal. Together, they scarcely presented the image of loving newlyweds, and she wondered a trifle wryly if they looked married.

Food was the last thing on her mind, and she ate mechanically, totally unappreciative of the superb seafood starter or the equally splendid lobster thermidor that followed. Even the champagne, Dom Perignon, suffered the sacrilege of being sipped seemingly without taste, and she declined both dessert and the cheeseboard in favour of strong aromatic black coffee.

Conversation between them verged on the banal, and Alyse heaved a mental sigh of relief when Aleksi indicated that they should leave if they were to keep their appointment with Hugh Mannering and the Department of Social Services.

'We'll take a taxi,' he said as they stepped out on to the pavement.

Within minutes he managed to hail one, and Alyse sat in silence, her gaze caught by the twin fitted rings adorning her left hand. The prismatic facets of a large solitaire diamond sparked blue and green fire in a brilliant burst from reflected sunlight, providing a perfect setting for its matching diamond-set wedding-ring.

'They suit you.'

Alyse glanced towards the owner of that drawling voice, and met his gaze without any difficulty at all. 'A simple gold band would have been sufficient,' she acknowledged with utter seriousness.

'No, it wouldn't.' There was an edge of mockery apparent, and she summoned up a dazzling smile.

'I forgot the *image* factor.'

He deigned not to comment, and it was something of a relief when the taxi cruised to a halt outside the building housing the solicitor's offices.

Fifty minutes later they summoned yet another taxi and instructed the driver to take them to the Family Services Department.

Bureaucratic red tape had a tendency to be time-consuming, with appointments rarely running to schedule, and today appeared no different. Consequently it was late afternoon before they emerged into the cool winter sunlight.

'A celebratory drink?'

There was a wealth of satisfaction in knowing that the initial legalities surrounding Georg's pending adoption were now officially in place, and Alyse found herself tilting her head as she met Aleksi's penetrating gaze. Quite without reason she found herself feeling slightly breathless, and desperately in need of a few hours away from his disturbing presence.

'There are still quite a few things I have to do.' Nothing of drastic importance, but he didn't need to know that. 'Could we combine it with dinner?'

'I'll organise yours and Georg's combined luggage and have it sent to the hotel. I'm sure the babysitter won't object to a change of venue.'

Her eyes widened in surprise, then long lashes swept down to form a protective veil. 'Is that really necessary?' she managed with remarkable steadiness, and detected cynicism in his drawling response.

'For the purpose of convention, we'll begin our marriage together by sharing the same roof. It's the hotel, or your home. Choose.'

'Just as long as you understand it won't involve the same bed.'

'Did I suggest that it would?'

Alyse closed her eyes, then slowly opened them again. Careful, a tiny voice cautioned. 'In comparison, I'm sure your luggage is far less substantial than Georg's and mine combined,' she declared in stilted tones, and watched as he hailed a taxi and instructed the driver to take them to his hotel.

His suite was situated on the twelfth floor and offered a magnificent view of the river. Alyse crossed the deep-piled carpet to stand at the window, all too aware of the intimacy projected by the opulently spreaded king-size bed.

'Help yourself to a drink,' Aleksi directed. 'The bar-fridge is fully stocked, and there's tea and coffee.' Without waiting for her reply, he moved towards the bedside phone and lifted the receiver, stating his intention to check out.

Anything remotely alcoholic would go straight to her head. 'I'd prefer coffee,' she said as he replaced the receiver, and good manners were responsible for her asking, 'Will you have some?'

When it was made, she sipped the instant brew appreciatively while Aleksi emptied contents of drawers and wardrobe into a masculine-styled bag. It was a chore he executed with the deft ease of long practice, and when it was completed he drained his coffee in a few measured swallows.

'Shall we leave?'

Alyse stood to her feet at once and preceded him from the suite, aware of an increasing sense of trepidation as she walked at his side.

It couldn't be fear, she analysed as they rode the lift down to the ground floor, for she wasn't afraid of him. Yet in some strange way he presented a threat, for she was aware of an elemental quality apparent, a primeval recognition that raised all her fine body hairs in protective self-defence.

It was after five when they reached suburban Peppermint Grove, and Alyse was grateful for the babysitter's presence as she effected the necessary introductions before escorting Aleksi to one of the spare bedrooms.

'You can leave your bag here. I'll make up the bed later.'

She felt awkward and ill at ease, and her chin tilted slightly as she met his mocking gaze. Damn you, she longed to scream at him. I *hate* you!

'I'll check on Georg.' Without another word she turned and left the room, telling herself she didn't care whether he followed her or not.

Georg was fast asleep, and Alyse moved silently towards her own bedroom, where she quickly shed her shoes, then exchanged her suit for a towelling robe.

Despite the babysitter's being hired until late evening, Alyse wanted to bath and feed Georg herself before settling him down for the night. It was a ritual she adored, and tonight it held special meaning, for only due legal process separated Georg from being officially hers.

Almost on cue she heard his first wakening cry, and she reached him within seconds, loving the way his tears ceased the moment she picked him up.

Bathing and feeding took almost an hour, and Alyse was supremely conscious of Aleksi's presence during the latter thirty minutes.

'May I?'

With extreme care she placed Georg into the crook of Aleksi's arm, watching every movement with the eagle eye of a mother-hen.

'I won't drop him,' Aleksi drawled with hateful cynicism, and her eyes darkened to a deep cerulean blue.

'I never imagined you would,' she snapped, aware that the babysitter was in the kitchen preparing her own dinner and therefore happily in ignorance of their barbed exchange.

Alyse willed Georg to cry, thus signalling his displeasure at being placed in a stranger's care, but he failed to comply and merely lay still, his bright eyes wide and dark. One could be forgiven for imagining he was fascinated, and perhaps he was, she decided uncharitably, for there had to be an awareness of change from her own scent and body-softness in comparison with his uncle's muscularly hard male-contoured frame.

Aleksi's expression was inscrutably intent, and she watched as he placed a forefinger into Georg's baby palm, detecting a momentary flaring of triumph as tiny fingers closed around it.

'He's a beautiful child,' she said quietly, and suffered Aleksi's swift scrutiny.

'He's my brother's son.' He paused slightly, then added with soft emphasis, '*Our* son.'

For some reason a chill shiver feathered its way down her spine. His words sounded irrevocable, almost as if he was issuing a silent warning. Yet he could have no inkling of her intention to instigate a divorce and gain custody of Georg—could he?

Stop it, she bade silently. You're merely being fanciful.

'He really should go down for the night.' She purposely shifted her gaze to Georg, who in total contrariness looked as if he had every intention of remaining wide awake.

'Why don't you go and change?' Aleksi suggested. 'The babysitter can settle him into his cot, and you can check him before we leave.'

A slight frown momentarily furrowed Alyse's brow.

'Dinner,' he elaborated.

The thought of suffering through another meal in his sole company was the last thing she wanted, but the alternative of staying in was even worse.

'I'm not very hungry, and I still have to pack.' It was a token protest at best, and he knew it.

'We won't be late.'

Dammit, what she'd give to ruffle that implacable composure! A sobering thought occurred that she *had*, and the result wasn't something she'd willingly choose to repeat.

'In that case, I'll go and get ready.'

'Unequivocal compliance, Alyse?'

'Conditional accedence,' she corrected, and leaning forward she brushed her lips to Georg's forehead. 'Goodnight, darling,' she bade softly. 'Sleep well.'

The gesture brought her far too close to Aleksi, and she straightened at once, moving away without so much as a backward glance as she left the room.

Selecting something suitable to wear took scant minutes, and she chose to freshen her make-up, merely adding a light dusting of powder and re-applying lipstick before running a brush through her hair.

Slipping into shoes, she collected a clutch-purse, then took one quick glance at her mirrored reflection, uncaring that the tailored black dress and red jacket provided a striking foil for her attractive features and pale shining hair.

As she emerged from her room she almost collided with Aleksi, and she bore his scrutiny with equanimity.

'Georg is already fast asleep,' he enlightened her quietly as he walked at her side to the lounge.

'Aleksi has written down the name and telephone number of the restaurant in case of any emergency,' the babysitter revealed, her eyes sparkling as they moved from one to the other, and Alyse could have sworn there was a degree of wistful envy in the young girl's expression. 'Please enjoy yourselves, and stay as long as you want. I don't mind.'

One glance at Aleksi Stefanos had been sufficient for the romantic eighteen-year-old to weave an impossible imaginary fantasy that bore no similarity whatsoever to reality!

Alyse could only proffer a sweet smile and utter her thanks, although inwardly she felt like screaming in vexation.

'Save it until we're in the car,' murmured Aleksi as he stood aside for her to precede him from the house, and she turned towards him with the smile still firmly pinned in place.

'Thus preserving the required image, I suppose?'

His gaze was full of mockery. 'Of course.'

Her expression registered an entire gamut of emotions, and she struggled to contain them as she slid into the passenger seat. 'Oh, go to hell!'

'I would advise putting a curb on your tongue.' His voice was dangerously soft, and in the dim interior of the car it was impossible to determine his expression. Not that she cared, she assured herself. He could bring down the wrath of a veritable Nemesis on her head, and it wouldn't matter at all.

The restaurant Aleksi had chosen was intimate, and offered superb cuisine. As a perfect complement, he ordered a bottle of Cristal, and proposed a solemn toast to their future together.

It wasn't something Alyse coveted, and she merely sipped the excellent champagne and forked morsels of food into her mouth with seemingly mechanical regularity.

Consequently it was a relief when coffee was served, and she breathed a silent sigh as Aleksi summoned the waiter for their bill.

In the car she sat in silence, grateful that he made no attempt at idle conversation, and the moment they arrived home she moved indoors with indecent haste, paid the babysitter and presented her with a parting gift, forcing a smile as the girl gave her an impulsive hug and bestowed her best wishes on them both.

'I'll make up your bed,' Alyse declared minutes after Anna's departure, 'then finish packing.'

'If you retrieve the necessary bed-linen, I'm sure I can manage,' Aleksi drawled, and she retaliated with deliberate sarcasm,

'A domesticated husband—how nice! Can you cook too?'

'Adequately. I also iron.'

'It almost seems too much!'

'Me, or my—abilities?' Aleksi's emphasis was deliberate, and she directed him an arctic glare.

'As I haven't experienced any of your abilities, I'm hardly in a position to comment.'

'Is that an invitation?'

His sarcasm was the living end. 'You know damn well it's not!' She moved quickly past him into the hallway and flung open the linen closet. 'You should have stayed at the hotel,' she declared, and was utterly incensed when she glimpsed his silent humour.

'Alone?' Aleksi mocked.

Alyse closed her eyes, then opened them again in a gesture of pure exasperation. 'Take a clean towel with you if you want to shower. Goodnight,' she added pointedly. Without a further word she walked towards her bedroom, then went in and closed the door behind her.

If he dared to follow her, she'd do him a mortal injury, she determined vengefully as she set about filling a suitcase with the remainder of her clothes. When the chore was completed she looked in on Georg, then crept back to her room, undressed, and slipped into bed.

She was so tired she should have fallen asleep within minutes, except there were fragmented images torturing her subconscious mind, the most vivid of which was the compelling form of Aleksi Stefanos. He appeared as a dark, threatening force: compelling, and infinitely powerful.

She had married in haste, out of love and loyalty to her sister and baby Georg. Would she repent at leisure, transported several thousand kilometres to the opposite side of the continent, where Aleksi Stefanos was in command?

Alyse found it impossible not to feel apprehensive as she boarded the large Boeing jet the following morning, and as each aeronautical mile brought them steadily closer to their destination the anxiety intensified.

A stopover in Melbourne and change in aircraft was instrumental in the final leg of their flight, and Alyse followed Aleksi into the arrival lounge at Coolangatta, aware that Georg, who had travelled surprisingly well, was now wide awake and would soon require the bottle the airline stewardess had kindly heated prior to disembarking.

Aleksi gave every appearance of being a doting uncle—*father*, she corrected silently, incredibly aware that he exuded dynamic masculinity attired in dark casual-style trousers, pale shirt and impeccably designed jacket that served to emphasise his breadth of shoulder—and she mentally squared her own, tilting her chin fractionally as he moved forward to lift various items of their luggage from the carousel and load them on to a trolley.

'I arranged to have my car brought to the airport,' he told her as Georg broke into a fractious wail. 'Wait here while I collect it from the car park.'

Alyse nodded in silent acquiescence, her entire attention caught up by the baby in the carrycot, whose tiny legs began to kick in vigorous rejection of what she suspected was a freshly soiled nappy.

By the time Aleksi returned Georg was crying lustily, and she opted to care for the baby's needs while Aleksi dealt with the luggage.

'Forceful young fellow,' Aleksi drawled minutes later as he eased the large BMW away from the terminal.

'Who's obviously intent on continuing in the same domineering vein as his forefathers,' Alyse offered sweetly as she gave Georg his bottle.

'Of whom you know very little,' reproved Aleksi, shooting her a quick mocking glance via the rear-view mirror, and she was quick with a loaded response.

'Oh, I wouldn't say that. I'm learning more each day.' She deliberately focused her attention on Georg, pacing the baby's attempt to drain the contents of his bottle in record speed, then when he had finished she burped him and laid him down in the carrycot, watching anxiously until he lapsed into a fitful doze.

Alyse pretended an interest in the darkened scenery beyond the windscreen, viewing the clearly lit highway and abundance of neon signs with apparent absorption.

'Is this your first visit to the Gold Coast?' he asked.

She turned towards him, glimpsing strength of purpose in features made all the more arresting by reflected headlights in the dim interior of the car.

'My parents brought Antonia and me here for a holiday about ten years ago,' she revealed.

The tiny lines fanning out from his eyes became more pronounced and his mouth widened into a slight smile. 'You'll notice a lot of changes.'

'For the better, I hope?'

'That would depend on whether you prefer the relaxed, casual holiday atmosphere the locals enjoyed all year round with only the inconvenience of visiting tourists during peak season, or the bustling commercial centre Surfers' Paradise has now become.'

'I guess one has to admit it's progress,' Alyse opined as the luxurious vehicle purred swiftly north along the double-lane highway.

'There's been a massive injection of Japanese-controlled funds into the area—hotels, resorts, golf courses,' Aleksi told her. 'The flow-on has resulted in a building boom: houses, shopping centres, high-rise developments, offices.'

'As a builder, you must be very pleased with the increased business.' It was a non-committal comment, and not meant to be judgemental.

However, it earned her a quick piercing glance before the road reclaimed his attention.

'The Coast has a long history of boom-and-bust cycles in building and real estate. Only the foolish choose to disregard facts and fail to plan ahead.'

No one in their right mind could call Aleksi Stefanos a fool, Alyse thought wryly. Remembering the force of his kiss, the steel-like strength of his arms as they had held her immobile, provided a vivid reminder of what manner of man she intended playing against. Yet it was a game she must win.

As the BMW pulled into the outer lane and sped swiftly past a line of slower-moving vehicles with ease, Alyse could only wonder at its horsepower capacity. There were outlines of densely covered hills reaching into the distance as Aleksi veered inland from the coastal highway.

'Sovereign Islands comprises a number of bridge-linked residentially developed islands situated to the east of Paradise Point, less than an hour's drive from the airport,' he told her. 'It's a prestigious security-guarded estate, and accessible by road from the mainland via a private bridge. Every home site has deep-water anchorage.'

'A gilded prison for the fabulously wealthy, with a luxury vessel moored at the bottom of every garden?'

'The residents prefer to call it civilised protection, and are prepared to pay for the privilege.'

'Suitably cushioned from the harsh realities of life.' Alyse couldn't believe she was resorting to sarcasm. It simply wasn't her style. Yet for some unknown reason the man behind the wheel generated the most adverse feelings in her, making her want to lash out against him in every possible way.

He didn't bother to reply, and she sat in silence, aware of an increasing anxiety as the car sped steadily north. Her home in Perth seemed a million kilometres away; the relative ease of life as she'd known it equally distant.

Her marriage was one of necessity, and merely mutually convenient. So why was she as wound up as a tightly coiled spring?

'We're almost there,' Aleksi declared drily, and Alyse spared her surroundings a swift encompassing glance, noting the numerous brightly lit architect-designed homes and established well-kept grounds.

Aleksi had said his home was a showcase, and she silently agreed as he turned the car on to a tiled driveway fronting a magnificent double-storeyed residence that seemed far too large for one man alone.

Pale granite walls were reflected by the car's powerful headlights, their lines imposing and classically defined. At a touch of the remote control module the wide garage doors tilted upwards, and Aleksi brought the BMW to a smooth halt alongside a Patrol four-wheel-drive vehicle.

Minutes later Alyse followed him into a large entrance foyer featuring a vaulted ceiling of tinted glass. A magnificent chandelier hung suspended from its centre, lending spaciousness and an abundance of light reflected by off-white walls and deep-piled cream-textured carpet. The central focus was a wide double staircase leading to the upper floor.

Wide glass-panelled doors stood open revealing an enormous lounge furnished with delicately carved antique furniture, and there were several carefully placed oil paintings gracing the walls, providing essential colour.

'I suggest you settle Georg,' said Aleksi as he brought in the luggage. His expression was a inscrutable mask as he chose a passageway to his left, and Alyse had little option but to follow in his wake.

'The master suite has an adjoining sitting-room overlooking the canal——' with a wide sweep of his arm he indicated a door immediately opposite '—an en suite bathroom, and, to the left, a changing-room with two separate walk-in wardrobes.'

The décor had an elegance that was restful and visually pleasant, utilising a skilful mix of pale green and a soft shade of peach as a complement to the overall cream.

'There's the requisite nursery furniture in the sitting-room,' he continued, moving forward. 'And a spare bed which you can use until——'

'Until—*what*?' Alyse's eyes blazed blue fire in an unspoken challenge.

'You're ready to share mine,' he drawled with imperturbable calm.

She was so incredibly furious that she almost shook with anger, and she failed to feel Georg stir in her arms, nor did she register his slight whimper in sleepy protest. 'That will be *never*!'

Dark eyebrows slanted above eyes that held hers in deliberate mocking appraisal. 'My dear Alyse,' chided Aleksi with chilling softness, 'surely you expect the marriage to be consummated?'

Her eyes widened with angry incredulity. 'In a house this large, there have to be other adequate bedrooms from which I can choose.'

'Several,' Aleksi agreed. 'However, this is where you'll stay.'

Her chin tilted in a gesture of indignant mutiny. 'The hell I will!'

'Eventually you must fall asleep.' He gave a careless shrug as he indicated the large bed. 'When you do, I'll simply transfer you here.'

'You unspeakable fiend!' she lashed out. 'I won't let you do that.'

'How do you propose to stop me?'

His expression was resolute, and only an innocent would fail to detect tensile steel beneath the silky smoothness of his voice.

Alyse's heart lurched painfully, then skipped a beat. Only a wide aperture separated the sitting-room from the bedroom, with no door whatsoever to afford her any privacy.

'You're an unfeeling, insensitive——' She faltered to a furious halt, momentarily lost for adequate words in verbal description. '*Brute!*'

Something flickered in the depths of his eyes, then it was successfully masked. 'I suggest you settle Georg before he becomes confused and bewildered by the degree of anger you're projecting.' He turned towards the bedroom door. 'I'll be in the kitchen, making coffee.'

Alyse wanted to throw something at his departing back, and the only thing that stopped her was the fact that she held Georg in her arms.

Experiencing momentary defeat, she turned towards the sitting-room, seeing at a glance that it was sufficiently large to hold a pair of single chairs and a sofa, as well as a bed and nursery furniture.

Placing the baby down into the cot, she gently covered him, lingering long enough to see that he was asleep before moving back into the bedroom.

Defiance emanated from every pore in her body as she retrieved her nightwear from her bag. A shower would surely ease some of her tension, she decided as she made her way into the luxuriously fitted bathroom. Afterwards she'd beard Aleksi in the kitchen and reaffirm her determination for entirely separate sleeping quarters for herself and Georg.

It was heaven to stand beneath the jet of pulsating hot water, and she took her time before using one of several large fluffy bathtowels to dry the excess moisture from her body. Her toilette completed, she slipped on a nightgown and added a matching robe.

There were bottles to sterilise and formula to make up in case Georg should wake through the night, and, collecting the necessary carry-bag, she went in search of the kitchen.

She found it off a passageway on the opposite side of the lounge, and she studiously ignored the tall dark-haired man in the process of pouring black aromatic coffee from a percolator into one of two cups set out on the servery.

Luxuriously spacious, the kitchen was a delight featuring the latest in electronic equipment, and in normal circumstances she would have expressed pleasure in its design.

'I'm sure you'll find whatever you need in the cupboards,' Aleksi drawled as he added sugar and a splash of whisky.

'Thank you.' Her words were stilted and barely polite as she set about her task.

'A married couple come in daily to maintain the house and grounds,' he informed her matter-of-factly. 'And a catering firm is hired whenever I entertain.'

'With such splendid organisation, you hardly need a wife,' she retorted, impossibly angry with him—and herself, for imagining he might permit a celibate cohabitation.

'Don't sulk, Alyse,' he derided drily, and she rounded on him with ill-concealed fury.

'I am not *sulking*! I'm simply too damned angry to be bothered conducting any sort of civilised conversation with you!' With tense movements she put the newly made formula in the refrigerator.

'The bedroom arrangement stays,' Aleksi declared with hard inflexibility, and her eyes became brilliant blue pools as she stood looking at him, refusing to be intimidated by his powerful height and sheer indomitable strength.

'All hell will freeze over before I'll willingly share any bed you happen to occupy!'

A faint smile tugged the edges of his mouth, and the expression in his eyes was wholly cynical. 'Why not have some coffee?' he queried mildly, and Alyse was so incensed by his imperturbable calm that she refused just for the sheer hell of opposing him.

'I'd prefer water.'

He shrugged and drained the contents of his cup. 'I'll be out most of tomorrow, checking progress on a number of sites, consulting with project managers. I've written down the name and phone number of a highly reputable babysitter in case you need to go out, and I'll leave a set of keys for the house and the car, together with some money in case there's anything you need.'

'I have money of my own,' she declared fiercely, and saw one eyebrow lift in silent quizzical query.

'Call it a housekeeping allowance,' Aleksi insisted as he leaned against the servery. 'And don't argue,' he warned with dangerous softness.

Without a further word she turned and filled a glass with chilled water, then drank it. With head held high she crossed the kitchen, her expression one of icy aloofness. 'I'm going to bed.' It was after eleven, and she was weary almost beyond belief.

'I'll show you how to operate the security system,' he insisted, straightening to his full height.

Five minutes later she entered the master suite, aware that he followed in her wake. Her back was rigid with silent anger as she made her way through to the sitting-room, and once there she flung off her robe, slid into bed, closed her eyes and determinedly shut out the muted sound of the shower operating in the en suite bathroom.

Much to her annoyance she remained awake long after the adjoining bedroom light was extinguished, and lay staring into the darkness, incredibly aware of Aleksi's proximity.

She hated him, she denounced in angry silence. *Hated* him. Why, he had to be the most damnable man she'd ever had the misfortune to meet. Indomitable, inflexible, *impossible*!

She must have slept, for she came sharply awake feeling totally disorientated and unsure of her whereabouts for a brief few seconds before memory surfaced, and she lay still, willing conscious recognition for the sound which had alerted her subconscious mind.

Georg? Perhaps he was unsettled after the long flight and restless in new surroundings.

Slipping cautiously out of bed, she trod silently across the room to the cot, her eyes adjusting to the reflection of the low-burning nightlight as she anxiously inspected his still form.

Wide eyes stared at her with unblinking solemnity, and Alyse shook her head in smiling admonition. With practised ease she changed his nappy, then covered him, only to hear him emit a whimpering cry.

Within seconds it became an unrelenting wail, and, quickly flinging on a wrap, she picked him up, murmuring softly as she cradled him.

'Problems?'

Alyse turned in startled surprise at the sound of Aleksi's voice so close behind her. 'He's only very recently started missing a late-night feed,' she told him quietly. 'I think the flight may have unsettled him.'

'Give him to me while you heat his bottle.'

'I can easily take him into the kitchen, then you won't be disturbed.'

'Go and do it, Alyse,' drawled Aleksi, calmly lifting Georg from out of her arms.

Her chin tilted fractionally as she met his unequivocal gaze, then just as she was about to argue the baby began to cry in earnest and, defeated, she stepped past Aleksi and made her way from the bedroom, fumbling occasionally as she searched for elusive light switches.

The tap emitted hot water at a single touch. *Boiling* hot, she discovered, biting her lips hard against a shocked curse as she withdrew her scalded hand. Ignoring the stinging pain, she warmed a bottle of prepared formula, then hurried back to the bedroom.

Aleksi was sitting on the edge of the bed cradling the tiny infant, and Alyse experienced a shaft of elemental jealousy at his complete absorption.

She wanted to snatch Georg out of his arms and retreat from the implied intimacy of the lamplit room with its large bed and the dynamic man who seemed to dominate it without any effort at all.

'I'll take him now,' she declared firmly, and her hand brushed his as she retrieved the baby, sending an electric charge through her veins.

Sheer dislike, she dismissed as she tended to Georg's needs, and on the edge of sleep she took heart in the fact that she would have most of the day to herself. A prospect she found infinitely pleasing, for without Aleksi's disturbing presence she could explore the house at will, even swim in the pool while Georg slept. And attempt to come to terms with a lifestyle and a husband she neither needed nor coveted.

CHAPTER FIVE

ALYSE entertained no qualms whatsoever as she followed Georg's pre-dawn routine. If Aleksi insisted that she and Georg occupy the master suite, then he could darned well suffer the consequences of sleep interrupted by a baby's internal feeding clock, she determined as she settled Georg after his bottle. Gathering up jeans, a warm long-sleeved sweater and fresh underwear, she crossed to the en suite bathroom and took a leisurely shower.

When she re-entered the bedroom Aleksi was in the process of sliding out of bed, and she hastily averted her eyes from an expanse of muscular flesh barely protected from total nudity by a swirl of bedlinen.

'Good morning.'

His drawled amusement put her on an immediate defensive, and her eyes lit with ill-disguised antagonism as she uttered a perfunctory acknowledgment on her way to the sitting-room.

Damn him! she cursed as she quickly straightened her bed, tugging sheets with more than necessary force. He possessed an ability to raise her hackles to such a degree that she was in danger of completely losing her temper at the mere sight of him!

Aleksi was already in the kitchen when she entered it some five minutes later, and she cast his tall rangy jeans-clad, black-sweatered frame the briefest of glances as she took a cup and filled it with freshly brewed coffee, blithely ignoring the fact that he was in the process of breaking eggs into a pan.

'Breakfast?'

She met his dark gaze with equanimity. 'It's barely six. I'll get something later.'

A newspaper lay folded on the servery and she idly scanned the headlines as she sipped the contents of her cup.

'There's an electronic device connected to the intercom system that can be activated to ensure that Georg is heard from any room in the house,' Aleksi told her.

'You were very confident of succeeding, weren't you?' Alyse couldn't help saying bitterly. 'The abundance of nursery furniture, toys—everything organised before you left for Perth.'

He skilfully transferred the contents from the pan on to a plate, collected toast and coffee and took a seat at the breakfast table.

His silence angered her immeasurably, and some devilish imp urged her along a path to conflagration. 'No comment?' she demanded.

He looked up, and she nearly died at the ruthless intensity of his gaze. 'Why indulge in senseless fantasy?'

'Don't you mean fallacy? Somehow it seems more appropriate.'

'Are you usually this argumentative so early in the morning? Or is it simply an attempt to test the extent of my temper?'

There could be no doubt he possessed one, and she cursed herself for a fool for daring to probe the limit of his control. Yet beneath that innate recognition was a determined refusal to be intimidated in any way.

'Do you have a problem with women who dare to question your opinion?' she countered, permitting one eyebrow to lift in a delicate arch. 'Doubtless all your female *friends*,' she paused with faint emphasis, 'agree with everything you say to a point of being sickeningly obsequious. Whereas I couldn't give a damn.'

'That's a sweeping generalisation, when you know nothing about any of my friends.'

'Oh, I'm sure there's any number of gorgeous socialites willing to give their all at the merest indication of your interest,' she derided. 'I wonder how they'll accept the news that you've suddenly plunged into matrimony and legally adopted a son?'

Aleksi subjected her to a long level glance. 'I owe no one an explanation for any decision I choose to make.' He picked up his cup and drained the last of his coffee. 'The keys to the BMW are on the pedestal table beside my bed.' He rose from the table with catlike grace. 'Enjoy your day.'

'Thank you,' Alyse responded with ill-concealed mockery, watching as he crossed the kitchen before disappearing down the hallway.

She heard the slight snap of a door closing, followed by the muted sound of an engine being fired and a vehicle reversing, then silence.

Suddenly the whole day lay ahead of her, and with at least three hours before Georg was due to waken again, she hurriedly finished her coffee and made her way towards the foyer.

Mounting the staircase, she slowly explored the four bedrooms and adjoining bathrooms, plus a guest suite, all beautifully furnished and displaying impeccable taste.

Returning downstairs, she wandered at will through the lounge, formal dining-room, guest powder-room, and utilities, and merely stood at the door leading into an imposing study, noting the large executive desk, computer equipment, leather chairs and an impressive collection of filing cabinets. There were also several design awards in frames on the wall, witness to Aleksi's success.

From there she moved towards the kitchen, discovering another flight of stairs leading from an informal family room down to a third level comprising a large informal lounge, billiard-room, gymnasium, and sauna. Wide glass sliding doors from the lounge and billiard-room led out on to a large patio and free-form swimming-pool.

The colour-scheme utilised throughout the entire home was a combination of cream and varying shades of pale green and peach, presenting a visually pleasing effect that highlighted modern architecture without providing stereotyped sterility.

A thorough inspection of the pantry, refrigerator and freezer revealed that there was no need to replenish anything for several days, and a small sigh of relief escaped her lips as she emptied cereal and milk into a bowl and sat down at the breakfast table with the daily newspaper.

Afterwards there was time to tidy the dishes before Georg was due to waken, and with determined resolve she moved through the master suite to the sitting-room and quietly retrieved her bags. She was damned if she'd calmly accept Aleksi's dictum and share the same suite of rooms!

It was relatively simple to transfer everything up-stairs, although as the day progressed a tiny seed of anxiety began to niggle at her subconscious.

Dismissing it, she set about preparing an evening meal of chunky minestrone, followed by chicken Kiev and an assortment of vegetables, with brandied pears for dessert.

It was almost six when Alyse heard Aleksi return, and her stomach began a series of nervous somer-saults as he came into the kitchen, which was totally ridiculous, she derided silently.

'I hardly expected such wifely solicitude,' he drawled, viewing her slight frown of concentration with amusement.

Alyse glanced up from stirring the minestrone and felt her senses quicken. He looked strong and vital, and far too disturbingly male for any woman's peace of mind.

Her eyes flashed him a glance of deep sapphire-blue before she returned her attention to the saucepan. 'Is there any reason why I shouldn't prepare a meal?'

'Of course not,' Aleksi returned smoothly as he leaned against the edge of the servery.

She could sense the mockery in his voice, and hated him for it. 'Stop treating me like a naïve nineteen-year-old!' she flung with a degree of acerbity.

'How would you have me treat you, Alyse?'

'With some respect for my feelings,' she returned fiercely.

'Perhaps you'd care to elaborate?'

It was pointless evading the issue, and besides, it was only a matter of time before he'd discover Georg's absence from the nursery.

She drew a deep breath, then released it slowly. 'I've moved my belongings into an upstairs bedroom.'

The eyes that lanced hers were dark and unfathomable.

'I suggest you move them back down again,' he drawled with dangerous silkiness.

'*No*. I refuse to allow you to play cat to my mouse by dictating my sleeping arrangements.'

'Is that what I'm doing?'

Oh, she could *hit* him! 'Yes! I won't be coerced to conform by a display of sheer male dominance.'

'My dear Alyse, you sound almost afraid. Are you?'

Now she was really angry, and sheer bravado forced her to counter, 'Do I look afraid?'

'Perhaps you should be. I don't suffer fools gladly.'

'What's that supposed to mean?'

At that precise moment a loud wail emitted through the monitor, and Alyse threw Aleksi a totally exasperated look.

'It's time for his bottle.'

'I'll fetch him while you heat it.'

Momentarily defeated, she retrieved a fresh bottle from the refrigerator and filled a container with hot water.

Aleksi was a natural, she conceded several minutes later as he caught up the bottle, took a nearby chair and calmly proceeded to feed Georg.

'He should be changed first,' Alyse protested, meeting those dark challenging eyes, and heard him respond with quiet mockery,

'I already have.'

There was little she could do except give a seemingly careless shrug and return her attention to a variety of saucepans on the stove, although it rankled that he should display such an adeptness when she had so readily cast him into an entirely different mould.

Alyse settled Georg in his cot while Aleksi had a shower, and it was almost seven when they sat down to dinner.

'This is good,' he remarked.

Alyse inclined her head in silent acknowledgment. 'What would you have done if I hadn't prepared a meal?'

His gaze was startlingly direct. 'Organised a babysitter, and frequented a restaurant.'

'I mightn't have wanted to go.'

'Perversity, Alyse, simply for the hell of it?'

She couldn't remember arguing with anyone, not even Antonia at her most difficult. Yet something kept prompting her towards a confrontation with Aleksi at every turn, and deep within some devilish imp danced in sheer delight at the danger of it all.

'No comment?' he queried.

She met his gaze with equanimity. 'I have a feeling that anything I say will be used against me.'

'Perhaps we should opt for a partial truce?'

She was powerless to prevent the wry smile that tugged at the edges of her mouth. 'Would it last?'

'Probably not,' Aleksi agreed with a degree of cynicism. 'However, I'd prefer that we at least project an outward display of civility in the company of my parents.'

'Why? They know the reason for our marriage, and are aware it isn't an alliance made in heaven.' Alyse sipped from a glass of superb white wine. 'If you expect me to indulge in calculated displays of affection, forget it.'

He spooned the last of his minestrone, then waited for her to finish.

'I'd prefer to help myself,' Alyse said at once, knowing he'd serve her a far too generous portion. She wasn't very hungry, and merely selected a few vegetables, then toyed with dessert.

'There are numerous friends and business associates who will be anxious to meet you, and a party next Saturday evening will provide an excellent opportunity.' He leaned back in his chair and surveyed her with a veiled scrutiny. 'I'll organise the caterers.'

She got to her feet and began stacking plates, unable to prevent a flaring of resentment as he lent his assistance.

'I can manage,' she said stiffly, hating his close proximity within the large kitchen.

'I'll rinse, you can load the dishwasher,' Aleksi told her, and she gritted her teeth in the knowledge that his actions were deliberate.

'You now have a wife to take care of all this,' Alyse voiced sweetly. 'Why not relax in the lounge with an after-dinner port, or retire to your study?'

'So you can pretend I don't exist?'

Oh, he was too clever by far! '*Yes*, damn you.'

Dark eyes gleamed with ill-concealed humour. 'No one would guess a firebrand exists beneath that cool façade,' he mused cynically, causing her resentment to flare.

'I didn't possess a temper until you forced your way into my life!'

'*Forced*, Alyse?' he queried with soft emphasis. 'I've never had to coerce a woman into anything.'

His implication was intentional, and Alyse quite suddenly had had enough. Placing the plate she held carefully on to the bench, she turned and made to move past him.

'Since you obviously believe in equality, *you* finish the dishes. I'm going for a walk.'

'In the dark, and alone?'

Her eyes flared with brilliant blue fire. 'I need some fresh air, but most of all, I need a temporary escape from *you*!'

'No, Alyse.' His voice sounded like silk being razed by tensile steel, and she reacted without thought, hardly aware of her hand swinging in a swift arc until it connected with a resounding slap on the side of his jaw.

For a wild moment she thought he meant to strike her back, and she cried out as he caught hold of her hands and drew her inextricably close. Any attempt to struggle was defeated the instant it began, and after several futile minutes she simply stood in defiant silence.

Her pulse tripped its beat and measurably quickened at the degree of icy anger apparent. He possessed sufficient strength to break her wrists, and she flinched as he tightened his grasp. 'You're hurting me!'

'If you continue this kind of foolish behaviour, believe me, you *will* get hurt.'

His threat wasn't an idle one, yet she stood defiant beneath his compelling gaze. 'That's precisely the type of chauvinistic threat I'd expect you to make!'

With slow deliberation he released her wrists and slid his hands up to her shoulders, impelling her forward, then his mouth was on hers, hard and possessively demanding.

Alyse clenched her teeth against his intended invasion, and a silent scream rose and died in her throat beneath the relentless determined pressure. She began to struggle, flailing her fists against his arms, his ribs—anywhere she could connect in an effort to break free.

She gave a muffled moan of entreaty as he effortlessly caught hold of her hands and held them together behind her back—an action that brought her even closer against his hard masculine frame, and there was nothing she could do to prevent the hand that slid to her breast.

A soundless gasp escaped her lips as she felt his fingers slip the buttons on her blouse, then slide beneath the silk of her bra. She wanted to scream in outrage as his mouth forced open her own, and his tongue became a pillaging, destructive force that had her silently begging him to stop.

When he finally released her, she swayed and almost fell, and a husky oath burned her ears in explicit, softly explosive force.

Her lips felt numb and swollen, and she unconsciously began a tentative seeking exploration with the tip of her tongue, discovering ravaged tissues that had been heartlessly ground against her teeth.

Firm fingers lifted her chin, and her lashes swiftly lowered in automatic self-defence against the hurt and humiliation she knew to be evident in their depths.

Standing quite still, she bore his silent scrutiny until every nerve stretched to its furthest limitation.

'Let me go. Please.' She had to get away from him before the ache behind her eyes manifested itself in silent futile tears.

Without a word he released her, watching as she slowly turned and walked from the room.

The temptation to run was paramount, except where could she run to that he wouldn't follow? A hollow laugh choked in her throat as she ascended the stairs. Escape, even temporary, afforded her a necessary respite, and uncaring of Aleksi's objection to her move upstairs, she crept into Georg's room and silently undressed.

It wasn't fair—*nothing* was fair, she decided as she lay quietly in bed. Sleep was never more distant, and despite her resolve it was impossible not to dwell on the fact that the day after tomorrow Aleksi's parents would arrive. An event she wasn't sure whether to view with relief or despair.

A silent scream rose to the surface as she heard an imperceptible click, followed by the inward swing of the bedroom door. Anger replaced fright as she saw Aleksi's tall frame outlined against the aperture, and she unconsciously drew the covers more firmly about her shoulders.

She watched in horrified fascination as he crossed to the cot and carefully transferred Georg on to the bed beside her.

'What do you think you're doing?' she vented in a sibilant whisper.

'I imagine it's perfectly clear,' he drawled as he effortlessly picked up the cot and carried it from the room.

Within minutes he was back, and she stared in disbelief as he scooped the baby into his arms. At the door he turned slightly to face her.

'You can walk, or be carried,' he said quietly. 'The choice is yours.'

Then he was gone, and Alyse was left seething with helpless anger. *Choice?* What choice did she have, for heaven's sake! Yet she was damned if she'd meekly follow him downstairs and slip into bed, defeated.

With each passing second she was aware of her own foolishness; to thwart him was the height of folly, and would doubtless bring retribution of a kind she would be infinitely wise to avoid. Except that wisdom, at this precise moment, was not high on her list.

Fool, an inner voice cautioned. *Fool.* Haven't you suffered enough punishment already, without wilfully setting yourself up for more?

Even as she considered capitulation, Aleksi re-entered the room, and she held his narrowed gaze with undisguised defiance as he moved to the side of the bed.

Without a word he wrenched the covers from her grasp, then leant forward and lifted her into his arms.

Alyse struggled, hating the ease with which he held her. 'Put me down, you fiend!'

'I can only wonder when you'll learn that to oppose me is a totally useless exercise,' he said cynically, catching one flailing fist and restraining it with galling ease.

'If you're hoping for meek subservience, it will never happen!' Dear lord, he was strong; any movement she made was immediately rendered ineffectual.

'You'd have to be incredibly naïve not to realise there's a certain danger in continually offering resistance,' he drawled, and she momentarily froze as fear licked her veins.

'Sex, simply for the sake of it?' she queried, meeting his gaze with considerable bravery. 'How long did you allow me, Aleksi—two, three nights?'

She could feel his anger unfurl, emanating as finely tuned tension over which she had little indication of his measure of control. Her eyes blazed a brilliant clear blue, not crystalline sapphire but holding the coolness of lapis lazuli.

'Well, get it over and done with, damn you! Although I doubt if you'll gain much satisfaction from copulating with an uninterested block of ice!'

His eyes seemed incredibly dark, and his mouth assumed a cruelty that made her want to retract every foolish word. In seeming slow motion he released her down on to the floor in front of him, and she stood mesmerised as he subjected her to a slow, raking appraisal.

Her nightgown was satin-finished silk edged with lace and provided adequate cover, but beneath his studied gaze she felt positively naked. A delicate pink tinged her cheeks as his eyes lingered on the gentle swell of her breasts, then slid low to the shadowed cleft between her thighs before slowly returning to the soft curves beneath the revealing neckline.

Against her will, a curious warmth began somewhere in the centre of her being and slowly spread until it encompassed her entire body.

Reaching out, he brushed gentle fingers against her cheek, then let them drift to trace the contours of her mouth before slipping to the edge of her neck, where he trailed the delicate pulsing cord to examine with tactile sensuality the soft hollows beneath her throat.

Her eyes widened, but her gaze didn't falter as his hand slid to the soft curve of her breast and slowly outlined its shape between thumb and forefinger. When he reached the sensitive peak it was all she could do not to gasp out loud, and she suppressed a tiny shiver as he rendered a similar exploration to its twin.

Slowly and with infinite care, he slid his hand to the shoestring straps and slipped first one, then the other from her shoulders.

For what seemed an age he just looked at her, and she stood mesmerised, unable to gain anything from his expression. Then he lowered his head down to hers, and she tensed as his mouth took possession of her own.

Except that the hard, relentless pressure never eventuated, and in its place was a soft openmouthed kiss that was nothing less than a deliberate seduction of the senses.

His tongue began a subtle exploration, seeking out all the vulnerable ridges, the tender, sensitive indentations, before beginning a delicate tracery of the tissues inside her cheek.

He seemed to fill her mouth, coaxing something from her she felt afraid to give, and she released a silent groan of relief as his lips left hers to settle in one of the vulnerable hollows at the base of her throat.

Then she gave an audible gasp as she felt his lips slide down to her breast, and the gasp became a cry of outrage as he took the peak into his mouth and savoured it gently, letting his teeth graze the sensitised nub until she almost screamed against the myriad sensations he was able to evoke.

Oh, dear lord, what had she invited? To remain quiescent was madness, yet to twist out of his grasp would only prove that she was vulnerable to his potent brand of sensual sexuality.

Just when she thought she could stand it no longer, Aleksi shifted his attention to its twin, and she arched her neck, her whole body stretching like a finely tuned bow in the hands of a master virtuoso.

It wasn't until she felt his hand on her stomach that she realised her nightgown had slithered to a silken heap at her feet, and a despairing moan escaped her throat.

At that moment his head shifted, and his mouth resumed a provocative possession that took hold of her inhibitions and tossed them high, bringing a response that left her weak-willed and malleable.

Then it was over, and she could only look at him in helpless fascination as he slowly pushed her to arm's length.

His lips assumed a mocking curve as he taunted with dangerous softness. '*Ice*, Alyse?'

The sound of his voice acted like a cascade of chilled water, and her own eyes widened into deep blue pools, mirroring shame and humiliation. She crossed her arms in defence of her lack of attire, hating the warmth that coloured her cheeks, and there was nothing she could do to prevent the shiver that feathered its way across the surface of her skin.

Without a word he bent to retrieve her nightgown from the floor, slipped it over her head, then slid an arm beneath her knees.

She wanted to protest, except that there was a painful lump in her throat defying speech, and the will to fight had temporarily fled as each descending step down the elegant staircase brought her closer—*to what*? Sexual possession?

In the centre of the master bedroom he released her, setting her on her feet, and she stood hesitant, poised for flight like a frightened gazelle.

'Go to bed.'

Alyse reared her head in startled surprise, and her eyes felt huge in a face she knew to be waxen-pale.

'Yours,' Aleksi added with soft cynicism. 'Before I change my mind and put you in mine.'

Her lips parted, then slowly closed again. There wasn't a thing she could say that wouldn't compound the situation, so she didn't even try, choosing instead to walk away from him with as much dignity as she could muster.

Sleep proved an elusive entity, and she lay awake pondering whether his actions were motivated by cruelty or kindness. Somehow she couldn't imagine it to be the latter.

CHAPTER SIX

ALYSE chose to stay at home with Georg when Aleksi drove to collect his parents from Brisbane airport on the pretext that it would give them time alone together in which to talk. It would also give her the opportunity to prepare dinner.

As their expected arrival drew closer, Alyse became consumed with nerves, and even careful scrutiny of a family photograph did little to ease her apprehension.

Alexandros Stefanos was an older, more distinguished replica of his indomitable son, although less forbidding, and Rachel looked serene and dignified. Both were smiling, and Alyse wondered if they would regard her kindly.

She fervently hoped so, for she was infinitely more in need of an ally than an enemy.

After initial indecision over what to wear, Alyse selected a stylishly cut leather skirt and teamed it with a knitted jumper patterned in varying shades of soft blue and lilac.

It was late afternoon when the BMW pulled into the garage, and her stomach tightened into a painful knot at the sound of the door into the hall opening, followed by two deep voices mingling with a light feminine laugh.

Drawing in a deep breath, she released it slowly and made her way towards the foyer, where an attractive mature woman stood poised, looking every bit as apprehensive as Alyse felt.

Even as Alyse came to a hesitant halt, the older woman's mouth parted in a tentative smile, and her eyes filled with reflected warmth.

'Alyse,' she greeted quietly. 'How very nice to meet you.'

'Mrs Stefanos,' Alyse returned, unsure precisely how she should address her mother-in-law. The circumstances were unusual, to say the least!

'Oh, *Rachel*, please,' Aleksi's stepmother said at once, reaching forward to catch hold of both Alyse's hands. 'And Alexandros,' she added, shifting slightly to one side to allow her husband the opportunity to move forward.

It was going to be all right, Alyse decided as she submitted to Alexandros Stefanos's firm handshake. Perhaps some of her relief showed, for Aleksi spared her a reassuring smile that held surprising warmth.

'I'll take your luggage upstairs to the guest suite, then we'll have a drink,' he said.

'I'll give you a hand,' Alexandros indicated in a deeply accented voice, and Alyse turned towards Rachel.

'Come and sit down. Georg is due to wake soon.'

The older woman's eyes misted. 'Oh, my dear, you can't begin to know how much I want to see him!'

'He's beautiful,' Alyse accorded simply as she sank into a sofa close to the one Rachel had chosen.

'You love him very much.' It was a statement of fact, and Alyse's gaze was clear and unblinking.

'Enough not to be able to give him up. For Antonia's sake, as well as my own,' she added quietly.

An expression very much like sympathy softened Aleksi's stepmother's features—that, and a certain understanding. 'Aleksi is very much Alexandros's son,' she offered gently. 'Yet beneath the surface lies a wealth of caring. I know he'll be a dedicated father, and,' she paused, then added hesitantly, 'a protective husband.'

But I don't want a husband, Alyse felt like crying out in anguished rejection of the man who had placed a wedding band on her finger only days before. And if I did, I certainly wouldn't have chosen your diabolical stepson!

The sound of male voices and muted laughter reached their ears, and Alyse turned towards the men as they came into the lounge.

'A drink is called for,' declared Aleksi, moving across to the bar. 'Alexandros? Rachel?'

Somehow she had imagined an adherence to formality, and Aleksi's easy use of his parents' Christian names came as a surprise.

'Some of your Queensland beer,' Alexandros requested, taking a seat beside his wife. 'It's refreshingly light.'

'I'll have mineral water,' Rachel acknowledged with a faint smile. 'Anything stronger will put me to sleep.'

'Alyse?'

'Mineral water,' she told him, then turned to Rachel. 'Unless you'd prefer tea or coffee?'

'My dear, no,' the older woman refused gently. 'Something cold will be fine.'

Georg woke a few minutes later, his lusty wail sounding loud through the intercom system, and Alyse dispensed with her glass and hurriedly rose to her feet.

'I'll change him, then bring him out.' She met Rachel's anxious smile. 'Unless you'd like to come with me?'

'I'd love to,' the older woman said at once, and together they crossed the lounge to the hall.

By the time they reached the master bedroom Georg was in full cry, his small face red and angry.

'Oh, you little darling!' Rachel murmured softly as his cries subsided into a watery smile the instant he sighted them.

'He's very shrewd,' Alyse accorded, her movements deft as she removed his decidedly damp nappy and exchanged it for a dry one. 'There, sweetheart,' she crooned, nuzzling his baby cheek, 'all ready for your bottle.'

His feet kicked in silent acknowledgment, and Rachel gave a delighted laugh.

'Georgiou used to do that too.'

Alyse felt a pang of regret for the older woman's sorrow. 'Would you care to take him? I thought you might like to give him his bottle in the lounge.'

Rachel's eyes shimmered with unshed tears. 'Thank you.'

It was heart-wrenching to see the effect Georg had on his grandparents, and Alyse had to blink quickly more than once to dispel the suspicious dampness that momentarily blurred her vision.

An hour later the baby was resettled in his cot for the night, and Rachel retired upstairs to freshen up while Alyse put the finishing touches to dinner.

After much deliberation, she had elected to serve a chicken consommé, followed by roast chicken with a variety of vegetables, and settled on fresh fruit for dessert. Unsure of Alexandros's palate, she'd added a cheese platter decorated with stuffed olives and grapes.

The meal was a definite success, and with most of her nervousness gone Alyse was able to relax.

'Tomorrow you must rest,' Aleksi told his parents as they sipped coffee in the lounge. 'In the afternoon I'll drive you into town and settle you both into the apartment, then in the evening we'll dine out together.'

Startled, Alyse felt her eyes widen in surprise, and Rachel quickly intervened in explanation.

'Aleksi owns an apartment in the heart of Surfers Paradise. Alexandros and I will stay there until we leave for Sydney to visit with my sister, after which we'll return and spend the remainder of our holiday on the Coast.'

Her expression softened as Alyse was about to demur.

'*Yes*, my dear. We value our independence and respect yours. The circumstances regarding your marriage are unusual,' Rachel added gently. 'You and Aleksi need time together alone.'

Alyse wanted to protest that the marriage was only one of convenience, and would remain so for as long as it took for her to escape to Perth with Georg. Except that she wouldn't consider voicing the words.

'And now,' Rachel declared, standing to her feet, 'if you don't mind, we'll retire.' Her smile wavered slightly as it moved from her husband to her stepson. 'It's been a long trip, and I'm really very tired.'

Alyse rose at once. 'Of course.' Her heart softened at the older woman's obvious weariness. 'There's everything you need in your suite.'

'Thank you, my dear.'

It seemed good manners to walk at Aleksi's side as his parents made their way into the foyer, and it wasn't until Rachel and Alexandros were safely upstairs that she turned back towards the lounge.

'I'll make some more coffee,' Aleksi said smoothly. 'I have a few hours' work ahead of me in the study.'

'There's plenty left in the percolator,' Alyse said with a slight shrug. 'It will take a minute to reheat. I'll bring it in, if you like.'

With a curt nod he turned towards the study, and it was only a matter of minutes before she entered that masculine sanctum and set a cup of steaming aromatic brew on his desk.

He was seated, leaning well back into a comfortable leather executive chair, and he regarded her with eyes that were direct and faintly probing.

'What do you think of my parents?'

'I hardly know them,' she said stiffly, longing to escape. In the company of Rachel and Alexandros she had been able to tolerate his company without too much difficulty, but now they were alone she was acutely aware of a growing tension.

'You like Rachel.' It was a statement, rather than a query, which she didn't bother to deny. 'And my father?'

'He seems kind,' she offered politely, and saw his mouth curve to form a cynical smile.

'Far kinder than his son?'

Her polite façade snapped. 'Yes. *You* seem to delight in being an uncivilised tyrant!'

An eyebrow rose in sardonic query. 'Whatever will you come up with next?'

Her eyes flashed a brilliant blue. 'Oh, I'm sure I'll think of something!'

The creases at the corners of his eyes deepened. 'I have no doubt you will.'

The temptation to pick something up from his desk and throw it at him was almost irresistible, and her hands clenched at her sides in silent restraint as she turned towards the door.

'Goodnight, Alyse.'

His drawled, faintly mocking tones followed her into the hall, and she muttered dire threats beneath her breath all the way into the kitchen.

An hour later she lay silently seething in bed, plotting his figurative downfall in so many numerous ways that it carried her to the edge of sleep and beyond.

It was almost midday when Rachel and Alexandros came downstairs, coinciding with Aleksi's arrival home, and after a relaxing meal Rachel eagerly saw to her grandson's needs, gave him his bottle, then settled him down for the afternoon.

Over coffee there was an opportunity for Alyse to become better acquainted with Aleksi's stepmother, and it was relatively simple to fill in details of Antonia's life, although she was aware of Aleksi's seemingly detached regard throughout a number of amusing anecdotes.

'I have some photographs,' Alyse told her. 'Most of them are in albums which are somewhere in transit between here and Perth, but I brought a few snaps with me that you might like to see.'

They were pictures of Antonia laughing, beautiful and lissom with flowing blonde hair and a stunning smile.

'What about you, Alyse?' Aleksi asked quietly. 'Were all the snaps taken only of Antonia?'

'No. No, of course not,' she answered quickly. 'There didn't seem much point in bringing the others with me.'

His gaze was startlingly direct. 'Why not?' Humour tugged the edges of his mouth. 'I would have enjoyed seeing you as a child.'

'Perhaps I should insist that you drag out shots depicting your pubescent youth,' Alyse said sweetly, and heard Alexandros's deep laugh.

'He was all bones, so tall, and very intense. An exceptional student.'

'Yes, I'm sure he was,' Alyse agreed with a faint smile.

'At nineteen he filled out,' Rachel informed her, shooting Aleksi a faintly wicked grin, 'developing splendid muscles, a deep voice, and a certain attraction for the opposite sex. Girls utilised every excuse under the sun to practise their own blossoming feminine wiles on him.'

'With great success, I'm sure,' Alyse remarked drily, and heard his husky laugh.

'I managed to keep one step ahead of each of them.'

'Shattering dreams and breaking hearts, no doubt?' The words were lightly voiced and faintly bantering, but his eyes stilled for a second, then assumed a brooding mockery.

'What about your dreams, Alyse?' he countered, silently forcing her to hold his gaze.

She swallowed the lump that had somehow risen in her throat, aware that their amusing conversational gambit had undergone a subtle change. 'I was no different from other teenage girls,' she said quietly. 'Except that my vision was centred on a successful career.'

'In which young men didn't feature at all?'

How could she say that Antonia was a carefree spirit who unwittingly attracted men without the slightest effort, while Alyse was merely the older sister, a shadowy blueprint content to shoulder responsibility? Yet there had never been any feelings of resentment or jealousy, simply an acceptance of individual personalities.

'I enjoyed a social life,' she defended. 'Tennis, squash, sailing at weekends, and there was the cinema, theatre, dancing.' Her chin lifted fractionally as she summoned a brilliant smile. 'Now I have a wealthy husband who owns a beautiful home, and an adored adopted son.' Her eyes glittered, sheer sapphire. 'Most women would rate that as being the culmination of all their dreams.'

Aleksi's soft laugh was almost her undoing, and it was only his parents' presence that prevented her from launching into a lashing castigation.

'Shall I make afternoon tea?' It was amazing that her voice sounded so calm, and she deliberately schooled her expression into a polite mask as she rose to her feet.

In the kitchen she filled the percolator with water, selected a fresh filter, spooned in ground coffee and set it on the element. Her hands seemed to move of their own accord, opening cupboards, setting cups on to saucers, extracting sugar, milk and cream, then setting a cake she'd made that morning on to a plate ready to take into the lounge.

When the coffee was ready, she put everything on to a mobile trolley and wheeled it into the lounge, dispensing everything with an outward serenity that would, had she been an actress, have earned plaudits from her peers.

Conversation, as if by tacit agreement, touched on a variety of subjects but centred on none, and it was almost four o'clock when Aleksi rose to his feet with the expressed intention of driving Rachel and Alexandros into town.

'I'm looking forward to this evening, my dear,' Rachel declared as she slid into the rear seat of the car, and Alyse gave her a smile that was genuinely warm.

'So am I,' she assured her, then stood back as Aleksi reversed the BMW down the driveway.

Indoors, she quickly restored the lounge to order and then dispensed cups and saucers into the dishwasher before crossing to the bedroom for a quick shower. Georg would wake in an hour, and she'd prefer to settle him down for the night rather than leave him to the babysitter.

Selecting something suitable to wear was relatively simple, and she chose an elegant two-piece suit in brilliant red silk, opted against wearing a blouse, and decided on high-heeled black suede shoes and matching clutch-purse. Make-up was understated, with skilful attention to her eyes, then she blowdried her hair and slipped on a silk robe, confident that within five minutes of settling Georg she could be ready.

The sound of the front door closing alerted her attention, and seconds later Aleksi entered the room.

'The babysitter will be here at six,' he told her as he shed his jacket and tossed it on to the bed. 'We'll collect my parents at six-thirty, and our table is booked for an hour later.'

Alyse merely nodded as his fingers slid to the buttons on his shirt, and he paused, his eyes narrowing on her averted gaze.

'Is there some problem with that?'

'None at all,' she said stiffly.

'Don't indulge in a fit of the sulks,' Aleksi cautioned, and she rounded on him at once with all the pent-up fury she'd harboured over the past hour.

'I am not sulking!' she snapped angrily. 'I just don't care to be figuratively dissected, piece by piece, in the presence of your parents, simply as a means of amusement!'

One eyebrow arched, and his mouth assumed its customary cynicism. 'What, precisely, are you referring to?'

'I didn't sit at home while Antonia went out and had all the fun,' she told him, holding his gaze without any difficulty at all.

'But you assumed responsibility for her welfare, did you not?' Aleksi queried with deceptive mildness. 'And, as the eldest, shouldered burdens which had your parents been alive would have given you more freedom?'

'If you're suggesting I assumed the role of surrogate parent, you couldn't be more wrong!'

He stood regarding her in silence for what seemed an age. 'Then tell me what you did out of work hours, aside from keep house?'

Her eyes became stormy. 'I don't owe you any explanations.'

'Then why become defensive when I suggested you took the elder sister role so seriously?'

'Because you implied a denial of any social existence, which isn't true.'

'So you went out on dates, enjoyed the company of men?'

The desire to shock was paramount. 'Yes,' she said shortly, knowing it to be an extension of the truth. Her chin tilted slightly, and her eyes assumed a dangerous sparkle. 'What comes next, Aleksi? Do we each conduct a head-count of previous sexual partners?'

'Have there been so many?'

'I don't consider it bears any relevance to our relationship,' she said steadily, and saw his eyes narrow.

'Do you doubt my ability to please you?'

The conversation had shifted on to dangerous ground, and Alyse felt her stomach nerves tighten at the thought of that strong body bent over her own in pursuit of sexual pleasure.

'Are you suggesting we indulge in sex simply for the sake of it a mutual claim for conjugal rights?'

His eyes gleamed with sardonic humour. 'My dear Alyse, do you perceive sex merely as a duty?'

He lifted a hand and cupped her jaw, letting his thumb brush her cheek. 'Either your experience is limited or your lovers have been selfishly insensitive.'

It was impossible to still the faint rush of colour to her cheeks, and her eyes silently warred with his as she sought to control her temper.

Slowly he lowered his head, and she stood in mesmerised fascination as his lips caressed her temple, then slid down to trace the outline of her mouth in a gentle exploration that was incredibly evocative.

A faint quiver of apprehension ran through her body, and her mouth trembled as his tongue probed its soft contours, then slid between her lips to wreak sweet havoc with the sensitised tissues.

It would be so easy to melt into his arms and deepen the kiss. For a few timeless seconds Alyse ignored the spasms of alarm racing to her brain in warning of the only possible conclusion such an action would have.

A soft hiccuping cry emerged from the adjoining sitting-room, and within seconds Georg was in full swing, demanding sustenance in no uncertain terms.

'Pity,' murmured Aleksi as he released her, and her eyes widened, then clouded with sudden realisation as she turned quickly away from him.

Crossing into the sitting-room, she picked Georg up from his cot and changed him, then made her way to the kitchen where she heated his bottle and fed him.

He sucked hungrily, and she slowed him down, talking gently as she always did, sure that he was able to understand simply by the tone of her voice that he was very much loved. He seemed to grow with each passing day, and her heart filled with pride as she leant forward to brush her lips against his tiny forehead.

He was worth everything, *anything* she had to endure as Aleksi Stefanos's wife. A truly beautiful child who deserved to be cherished, she decided wistfully as she settled him almost an hour later.

Swiftly discarding her robe, she quickly donned the silk evening suit and slipped her feet into the elegant high-heeled suede shoes. A brisk brush brought her hair into smooth order, and she sprayed a generous quantity of her favourite perfume to several pulsebeats before standing back to survey the result in the full-length mirror.

Muted chimes sounded through the intercom, and Aleksi emerged from his dressing-room.

'That will be Melanie. She's a dedicated law student, the eldest of five, and extremely capable. I'll let her in.'

The breath caught in Alyse's throat at the sight of him, and she rapidly schooled her expression as she took in his immaculate dark suit, thin-striped shirt and impeccably knotted tie.

Any feelings of unease at leaving Georg with a total stranger were dispelled within minutes of meeting the girl Aleksi introduced as the daughter of one of his associates.

'I've written down the phone number of the restaurant,' he told her, handing over a slip of paper. 'And the apartment, in case we stop for coffee when we drop off my parents. We'll be home around midnight. If it's going to be any later, I'll ring.'

'Georg is already asleep,' Alyse added. 'I doubt if he'll wake, but if he does it's probably because he needs changing. If he won't settle, give him a bottle. He's just started sleeping through the night, except for the occasional evening. If you'll come with me, I'll show you where everything is.'

Fifteen minutes later she was seated in the luxurious BMW as it purred along the ocean-front road that led into the heart of Surfers Paradise.

'Where are we dining?' she asked.

'The Sheraton-Mirage; it's located on the Spit.'

'Where anyone important is *seen*, no doubt.' She hadn't meant to sound cynical, and she suffered his swift analytical glance as a consequence.

'Rachel fell in love with the resort complex when she and my father were here last year. It's at her request that we're dining there tonight.'

She should apologise, she knew, but the words refused to emerge, and she sat in silence until the car pulled to a halt at the entrance to a prestigious multi-storey apartment block overlooking the ocean.

At attendant slid in behind the wheel as Alyse followed Aleksi into the elegant foyer, and seconds later a lift transported them swiftly to an upper floor.

The apartment was much larger than she had expected, with magnificent views through floor-to-ceiling plate glass of the north and southern coastline. Pinpricks of light sparkled from a multitude of high-rise towers lining the coastal tourist strip, and beneath the velvet evening skyline the scene resembled a magical fairyland that stretched as far as the eye could see.

'You look stunning, my dear,' Rachel complimented Alyse quietly.

'Yes, doesn't she?'

Alyse heard Aleksi's faintly mocking drawl, and opted to ignore it. 'Thank you.'

'Would you prefer to have a drink here, or wait until we're at the complex?'

'The complex, I think,' Rachel concurred. 'I'm sure Alyse will be as enchanted with it as I am.'

A correct deduction, Alyse decided on entering the wide lobby with its deep-piled blue carpets, cream marble tiles and exotic antiques. The central waterfall was spectacular, as was the tiled lagoon with its island bar.

'We must come out during the day,' Rachel declared with a smile. 'The marina shopping complex directly across the road is delightful. We could explore it together, and share a coffee and chat.'

'My wife adores to shop,' Alexandros informed Alyse with a deep drawl not unlike that of his son.

They took a seat in the lounge-bar and Alyse declined anything alcoholic, aware of Aleksi's faintly hooded appraisal as she voiced her preference for an order identical to his stepmother's request for mineral water spiked with fresh orange juice.

'My dear, don't feel you must abstain simply because I choose to do so.'

'I don't drink,' she revealed quietly. 'Except for champagne on special occasions.'

'Dom Perignon?' queried Rachel with hopeful conspiracy, and Alyse smiled in silent acquiescence.

'In that case, we'll indulge you both at dinner,' said Aleksi, giving the waiter their order, then he sat well back in his chair, looking infinitely relaxed and at ease.

Alyse would have given anything to be rid of the nervous tension that steadily created painful cramps in her stomach. It was madness to feel so intensely vulnerable; insane, to be so frighteningly aware of the man seated within touching distance.

The image of his kiss, so warm and infinitely evocative, rose up to taunt her, and she had to summon all her reserves of willpower to present a smiling, seemingly relaxed façade.

No matter what private aspirations Rachel and Alexandros held for their son's marriage, it was apparent that the union afforded them tremendous pleasure. Equally obvious was an approval of their daughter-in-law, and Alyse experienced a feeling of deep regret—not only for Antonia's loss, but for her own. If she could have selected ideal parents-in-law, it would be difficult to choose a nicer couple than Aleksi's father and stepmother.

Such introspection was dangerous, and it was a relief when they entered the restaurant and were shown to their table.

CHAPTER SEVEN

THE setting was superb, the food a gourmet's delight, presented with flair and artistry. Except that Alyse's appetite seemed to be non-existent as she selected cream of mushroom soup, then followed it with crumbed prawn cutlets.

After sipping half a flute of champagne she felt more at ease, but she was supremely conscious of Aleksi's solicitous attention, the accidental brush of his fingers against her own, and the acute sensation that he was instigating a deliberate seduction.

Consequently it was a relief when Alexandros asked if she'd care to join him on the dance floor.

Alyse spared Rachel an enquiring smile. 'Do you mind?'

'Of course not, my dear.' Rachel's features assumed a faintly mischievous expression. 'Aleksi and I will join you.'

Alexandros, as Aleksi's father insisted she call him, was every bit as commanding as his indomitable son, Alyse decided as she rose graciously from the table and allowed him to lead her on to the restaurant's small dance floor. There was the same vital, almost electric energy apparent, an awareness of male sensuality that had little to do with chronological age. Alexandros Stefanos was charming: polite, deferential, and genuine. The sort of man a woman could entrust with her life.

'You're light on your feet, like a feather,' he complimented her. 'So graceful.'

'You're an accomplished partner,' she returned with a faint smile.

'And you're very kind.'

Am I? she thought silently. I'm not at all kindly disposed towards your son. Out loud, she said, 'I hope you and Rachel are enjoying your holiday.'

'My dear, how can I explain the joy among the grief in discovering that Georgiou had fathered a son? He's very much loved, that child, his existence so precious to us all.'

Alyse couldn't think of a single thing to say, and she circled the floor in silence, hardly aware of the music or their fellow dancers on the floor.

'Shall we change partners?' a deep voice drawled from close by, and she missed her step, distinctly ill at ease that she was about to be relinquished into the waiting arms of her husband.

Aleksi's hold was far from conventional, and she wanted to scream with vexation.

'Must you?' she hissed, totally enraged at the proprietorial possessiveness of his grasp. She was all too aware of a subjugation so infinite, it was impossible not to feel afraid.

'Dance with my wife?'

His resort to mockery was deliberate, and momentarily defeated in the knowledge that self-assertion would only cause a scene, Alyse tilted her head and gave him a brilliant smile.

'This is *dancing*, Aleksi? You can't begin to know how much I'd like to slap your face!'

One eyebrow slanted in cynical amusement. 'Good heavens, whatever will you do when we make love? Kill me?'

'I'll have a darned good try!'

His eyes darkened with ill-concealed humour. 'Yes, I do believe you will.'

There was no doubt he'd enjoy the fight, and its aftermath, while instinctive self-preservation warned that if she dared submit she would never be the same again.

The music playing was one of those incredibly poignant songs that stirred at the heartstrings, with lyrics of such depth that just hearing them almost brought tears to her eyes.

You're mad, she told herself shakily. You hate him, remember? The strain of the past few days; meeting Georg's grandparents. It was all too much.

A slight shiver feathered its way across the surface of her skin. Any kind of emotional involvement was a luxury she couldn't afford if she were to instigate a divorce and return to Perth with Georg.

'I'd like to go back to our table.' The words came out as a slightly desperate plea, and she strained away from him in her anxiety to escape the intimacy of his hold.

'The band will take a break soon. Besides, my parents are still dancing. We should return together, don't you think?' His voice sounded mild close to her ear, and she felt his breath stir at her temple, teasing a few tendrils of hair.

'I have the beginnings of a headache,' she improvised, and felt immeasurably relieved as he led her to the edge of the dance floor, his gaze sharp and far too discerning for her peace of mind.

'Fact, or fiction?'

Her eyes blazed a brilliant blue. 'Does it really matter?' Angry beyond belief, she turned and moved quickly away from him.

On reaching the brightly lit powder-room she crossed to an empty space in front of the long mirror and pretended interest in her features.

She was far too pale, she decided in analytical appraisal, and her eyes bore a vaguely haunted look, reflecting an inner tension that was akin to a vulnerable animal confronted by a hunting predator.

A tiny bubble of derisive laughter rose and died in her throat at her illogical parallel. Dear lord, she'd have to get a hold on herself. Imaginative flights of fancy were of no help whatsoever in her resolve against Aleksi Stefanos.

The invention of a headache wasn't entirely an untruth, for a persistent niggle began to manifest itself behind one eye, and she attributed its cause directly to her husband.

Aware that her escape could only be a temporary respite, she resolutely withdrew a lipstick from her evening purse and tidied her hair to its smooth bell-like style before returning to their table.

'My dear, are you all right?' Rachel asked the moment Alyse was seated, and she countered the force of three pairs of apparently concerned eyes with a reassuring smile.

'Yes, thank you.'

'You're very pale. Are you sure?'

Obviously she wasn't succeeding very well in the acting stakes! 'Georg still wakes through the night,' she explained lightly, 'and is often difficult to settle.'

'Georgiou was the same at a similar age—an angel by day, yet restless at night.' Rachel offered a conciliatory smile. 'It will soon pass.'

'Meanwhile it's proving quite disruptive to our sleep,' drawled Aleksi, shooting Alyse a particularly intimate glance.

Damn him, had he no shame? she fumed, forced into silence out of deference to his parents' presence.

'Tell me about the party you've both planned,' Rachel began, in what Alyse decided was a sympathetic attempt to change the subject.

'A delayed wedding reception,' Aleksi elaborated with bland disregard for her barely contained surprise. 'Providing an opportunity for family and friends to share the celebration of our marriage.'

Alyse felt her stomach execute a few painful somersaults. How dared he propose something so ludicrous? It was only compounding a mockery, and she wanted no part in it.

'What a wonderful idea!' his stepmother enthused, while Alyse sought to dampen an increasing sense of anger for what remained of the evening.

In the car she sat tensely on edge as Aleksi brought the luxurious vehicle to a smooth halt in the wide bricked apron at the entrance to the tall apartment block.

'Will you join us for coffee?' asked Rachel, and Alyse held her breath as Aleksi issued a reluctant refusal.

'It's quite late, and we're both anxious to get home.' His smile appeared genuinely warm. 'The babysitter is extremely capable, but it's the first time we've left Georg in her care.'

That was true enough, although it was unlikely that there had been any problems, and Alyse managed to smile as they bade each other good-night, issuing a spontaneous invitation for the older woman to join her the next day.

However, the instant the car cleared the driveway Alyse burst into angry pent-up speech.

'You are impossible!'

'Why, specifically?' Aleksi countered cynically, and she was so incensed that if he hadn't been driving she would have hit him.

Spreading one hand, she ticked off each consecutive grudge. 'Deliberately implying that we share the same bed. And when you announced a party, I hardly imagined you'd expect me to give a repeat performance as a blushing bride.'

'My dear Alyse, do you still blush?'

She cast him a furious glare. 'I used the term in a purely figurative sense.'

'Of course.'

'Oh, don't be so damned *patronising*!'

'If you want to fight, at least wait until we reach home,' he cautioned cynically, and, momentarily defeated, Alyse turned her attention to the passing scenery beyond the windscreen.

The sky was an inky black as it merged with the shallow waters of the inner harbour, providing a startling background for brightly lit venues along the famed tourist strip. Outlines were crisp and sharp, and a pinprick sprinkling of stars lent promise of another day of sunshine in a sub-tropical winterless climate.

Aleksi chose the waterfront road, and Alyse wondered darkly if he was deliberately giving her temper an opportunity to cool.

Georg hadn't even murmured, Melanie reported, accepting the notes Aleksi placed in her hand before departing with a friendly smile.

'I'll check Georg,' said Alyse hastily.

'An excuse to escape, Alyse?'

'No, damn you!'

His eyes gleamed with latent mockery. 'I'll make coffee. Liqueur and cream?'

Resentment flared as she turned to face him. 'I'm going to bed—I've done my duty for the evening. Goodnight.'

There was a palpable pause. 'You consider an evening spent with Rachel and my father a duty?'

Alyse closed her eyes, then opened them again. 'They're both utterly charming. Their son, however, is not.'

'Indeed?' His voice sounded like velvet-encased steel. 'Perhaps you would care to clarify that?'

'You act as if I'm your wife!'

One eyebrow rose in cynical query. 'My dear Alyse, I have in my possession a marriage certificate stating clearly that you are.'

'You know very well what I mean!'

'Does it bother you that I accord you a measure of husbandly affection?'

'Courteous attention I can accept,' she acknowledged angrily. 'But intimate contact is totally unnecessary.'

His smile was peculiarly lacking in humour. 'I haven't even begun with intimacy.'

Her hand flew in an upward arc, only to be caught in a bonecrushing grip that left her gasping with pain.

'So eager to hit out, Alyse? Aren't you in the least concerned what form of punishment I might care to mete out?' he asked deliberately, pulling her inextricably close.

'Do you specialise in wife-beating, Aleksi?' she countered in defiance, and suffered momentary qualms at the anger beneath the surface of his control.

'I prefer something infinitely more subtle,' he drawled, and she retaliated without thought.

'I hardly dare ask!'

'Sheer bravado, or naïveté?'

'Oh, *both*,' she acknowledged, then gave a startled gasp as he slid an arm beneath her knees and lifted her into his arms. 'What do you think you're doing?'

The look he cast her cut right through to her soul. 'Taking you to bed. Mine,' he elaborated with icy intent.

Her eyes dilated with shock. 'Don't! Please,' she added as a genuine plea to his sensitivity, rather than as an afterthought.

'You sound almost afraid,' he derided silkily.

Afraid I'll never be the same again, Alyse qualified silently, hating the exigent sexual chemistry that drew her towards him like a moth to flame.

'I hate you!' she flung desperately as he carried her through the lounge, and she was absolutely incensed at the speculative amusement apparent in the depths of his eyes.

In the bedroom he let her slide to her feet, and she was powerless to do anything other than stand perfectly still beneath his dark penetrating gaze.

'You react like an agitated kitten, all bristling fur and unsheathed claws.' His smile was infinitely sensual, his eyes dark and slumbrous as he took her chin between thumb and forefinger to tilt it unmercifully high. 'It will be worth the scratches you'll undoubtedly inflict, just to hear you purr.'

'Egotist,' she accorded shakily. 'What makes you think I will?'

He didn't deign to answer, and there was nothing she could do to avoid his mouth as it took possession of hers in a deliberately sensual onslaught that plundered the very depths of her soul.

With shocking ease he dispensed with her clothes, then his own, and she gave an agonised gasp as he reached for the thin scrap of lace-edged satin covering her breasts.

'Aleksi——'

'Don't?' he taunted softly, releasing the clasp and letting the bra fall to the carpet.

It was impossible to come to terms with a mixture of elation and fear, so she didn't even try, aware even as she voiced the protest that there could be no turning back. 'You can't mean to do this,' she said in agonised despair.

His hands cupped the creamy fullness of her breasts with tactile expertise, and the breath locked in her throat when his head descended and his mouth closed over one vulnerable peak. Sensation spiralled from the central core of her being, radiating through her body until she was consumed by an emotion so fiery, so damnably erotic, that it was all she could do not to beg him to assuage the hunger within.

His tasting took on a new dimension as he began to suckle, using his teeth with such infinite delicacy that it frequently trod a fine edge between pleasure and pain.

Just when she thought she could bear it no more, he relinquished his possession and crossed to render a similar onslaught to its twin.

Unbidden, her fingers sought the thickness of his hair, raking its well-groomed length in barely controlled agitation that didn't cease when he shifted his attention to her mouth and began subjecting that sensitive cavern to a seeking exploration that gradually became an imitation of the sexual act itself.

Alyse was floating high on a cloud of sensuality so evocative that it was all she could do not to beg him to ease the ache that centred between her thighs, and, as if he was aware of her need, his hand slid down to gently probe the sweet moistness dewing there.

Like a finely tuned instrument her body leapt in response, and she became mindless, an insignificant craft caught in a swirling vortex beyond which she had no control.

It wasn't until she felt the soft mattress beneath her back that realisation forced its way through the mists of desire, and she could only stare, her eyes wide with slumbrous warmth, as Aleksi discarded his shirt, then his trousers and finally the dark hipster briefs that shielded his masculinity.

There was a potent beauty in his lean well-muscled frame, a virility that sent the blood coursing through her veins in fearful anticipation, and she unconsciously raised her gaze to his, silently pleading as he joined her on the bed.

Her lips parted tremulously as his eyes conducted a lingering appraisal of their softly swollen contours, before slipping down to the rose-tipped breasts that burgeoned beneath his gaze as if in silent recognition of his touch.

Her limbs seemed consumed by languorous inertia, and she made no protest as he began a light, trailing exploration of her waist, the soft indentation of her navel, then moved to the pale hair curling softly between her thighs.

A sharp intake of breath changed to shocked disbelief as his lips followed the path of his hand in a brazen degree of intimacy she found impossible to condone.

Liquid fire coursed through her body, arousing each separate sensory nerve-end until she moaned an entreaty for him to desist. Except that nothing she said made any difference, and in a desperate attempt to put an end to the havoc he was creating she sank her fingers into his hair and tugged—*hard*.

It had not the slightest effect, and her limbs threshed in violent rejection until he caught hold of her hands and pinned them to her sides, effectively using his elbows to still the wild movements of her legs.

For what seemed an age she lay helpless beneath his deliberate invasion, hating him with a fervour that was totally unmatched, until, shifting his body weight, he effected a deep penetrating thrust that brought an involuntary gasp from her lips as delicate tissues stretched, then filled with stinging pain.

She was so caught up with it she didn't register the brief explicit curse that husked from Aleksi's throat, and she tossed her head from side to side to escape his mouth before it settled over hers, gentle, coaxing, and inflexibly possessive as she strove to free herself.

Without thought she balled her hands into fists and hit out at him, striking anywhere she could, then she became impossibly angry when it had no effect whatsoever.

The only weapons she had left were her teeth and her nails, and she used both, shamelessly biting his tongue, at the same time raking her nails down his ribcage, achieving some satisfaction from his harsh intake of breath.

'Witch,' he growled, lifting his mouth fractionally, and she cried out in agonised rejection.

'*Bastard!* I hate you, *hate* you, do you understand?'

His hands caught hers in a punishing grip and held them immobile above her head, and she began to struggle in earnest, fear lending her unknown strength as she fought to be free of him.

'Stop it, little fool,' he chastised, holding her with ease. 'You're only making it worse for yourself.'

Angry dark blue eyes speared his as she vented furiously, 'Get away from me, damn you!'

'Not yet.'

'Haven't you done enough?' It was a tortured accusation dredged up from the depths of her soul, and yet it failed to have the desired effect. 'Aleksi!' She would have begged if she had to, and it didn't help that he knew.

'Be still, little wildcat,' he soothed, easily holding both her hands with one of his as he gently pushed stray tendrils of hair back behind her ear. Then his mouth brushed her temple, pressed each eyelid closed in turn, before trailing down to the edge of her lips. With a touch as light as a butterfly's wing he teased their curved outline before slipping to the hollow at the base of her neck.

'Please don't.'

'What a contrary plea!' he murmured against her throat, and she could sense the smile in his voice. 'Just relax, and trust me.'

'Why should I?' she cried in an impassioned entreaty, only wanting to be free of him.

'The hurting is over, I promise.'

'Then why won't you leave me alone?' Her eyes seared his, then became trapped beneath the latent sensuality, the sheer animal magnetism he exuded, and almost in primeval recognition an answering chord struck deep within, quivering into hesitant life.

'This is why,' husked Aleksi, covering her mouth gently with his own as he began to move, slowly at first, creating a throbbing ache that swelled until she became caught up in the deep rhythmic pattern of his possession.

Impossibly sensuous, he played her with the skilled mastery of a virtuoso, bringing forth without any difficulty at all the soft startled cries of her pleasure, and the hands that had raked his flesh now cajoled in silent supplication as she accepted everything he chose to give.

The climax, when it came, was unexpected and tumultuous, an entire gamut of emotions so exquisite it defied description in that first initial experience, and afterwards she was too spent to attempt an accurate analysis.

With a return to normality came a degree of self-loathing, and the re-emergence of hatred for the man who had instigated her emotional catalyst. She became aware of her own body, the soft bruising inside and out, and the increasing need to escape, albeit temporarily, from the large bed and the indomitable man who occupied it.

'Where do you think you're going?'

It was difficult to stand naked before his gaze, although innate dignity lifted her head to a proud angle as she turned at the sound of that quiet drawling voice.

'To have a bath,' she responded evenly, and saw his eyes narrow fractionally before she moved towards the en suite bathroom.

Once inside, she closed the door, then pressed the plug into position in the large spa-bath and released water from the taps.

Within minutes steam clouded the room, and she added plenty of bath-oil to the cascading water before stepping into its warm depth.

Aleksi walked into the room as Alyse was about to reach for a sponge, and she was so incensed at his intrusion she threw the sponge without thought, watching as it connected with his chest.

His soft husky laughter as he calmly stepped into the bath to sit facing her was the last straw, and she flew at him in a rage, flailing her fists against his shoulders, his arms, anywhere she could connect, until he caught hold of her wrists with a steel-like grip.

'Enough, Alyse.' His voice was hard and inflexible, and she looked at him with stormy eyes, ready to do further battle given the slightest opportunity.

'Can't you see I want to be alone?' It was a cry from the heart, and to her horror she felt her lower lip tremble with damnable reaction. She was physically and emotionally spent, and there was the very real threat of tears as she determined not to let him see the extent of her fragility.

Eyes that were dark and impossibly slumbrous held her own captive in mesmerised fascination, and helpless frustration welled up inside her as her chin tilted at an angry angle. 'Must you look at me like that?'

'We just made love,' he drawled with latent humour. 'How would you have me look at you?'

'I hated it!' Alyse flung incautiously.

One eyebrow rose with sardonic cynicism. 'You hated the fact that it was *I* who awakened you to the power of your own sensuality.' His lips moved to form a twisted smile. 'And you hate yourself for achieving sexual pleasure with someone you profess to dislike.'

The truth of his words was something she refused to concede. 'You behaved like a barbaric—*animal*!'

'Who took his own pleasure without any concern for yours?' he demanded with undisguised mockery.

Colour stained her cheeks, and her lashes fluttered down to form a protective veil against his discerning scrutiny. 'I'll never forgive you,' she declared with quiet vehemence. *'Never.'*

'Spoken like an innocent,' Aleksi declared with sardonic amusement, and her eyes flew open to reveal shards of brilliant sapphire.

'Not any more, thanks to you!'

Lifting a hand, he brushed his fingers along the edge of her jaw. 'I'm almost inclined to query why.'

Alyse reared back from that light teasing touch as if it was flame, wanting to scream and rage against his deliberate seduction, the sheer force of his sensual expertise. Except she was damned if she'd give him the satisfaction. Instead, she said bitterly, 'I would have preferred a less brutal initiation.'

'Yet after the pain came pleasure, did it not?'

Her eyes glittered in angry rejection. 'Never having experienced anything to compare it with, I can't comment.'

His soft husky laughter was almost her undoing, and she stood to her feet, reached for a towel, then stepped quickly out of the bath, uncaring that he followed her actions.

It was then she saw the long scratches scoring his ribcage, and she turned away, feeling sickened that she could have inflicted such physical injury.

In the bedroom she collected her nightgown and donned it, then turned hesitantly as Aleksi entered the room.

'You'll sleep here with me, Alyse. And don't argue,' he added with quiet emphasis as her lips parted to form a protest.

Before she had the opportunity to move more than a few steps towards the sitting-room he had reached her side, and her struggles were ineffectual as he calmly lifted her into his arms and carried her to the large bed.

'I don't want to sleep with you,' she said fiercely, pushing against him as he slid in between the covers.

'Maybe not,' he drawled, settling her easily into the curve of his body. 'But I insist you do.'

'You damned dictatorial tyrant!'

'My dear Alyse, I can think of a far more pleasurable way to deploy your energy than by merely wasting it in fighting me.'

She froze at his unmistakable implication. 'I won't be used and abused whenever you——'

'Feel the urge?' he completed sardonically. 'I have a twelve-hour day ahead of me, and right now all I have in mind is a few hours' sleep. Unless you have other ideas, which I'll gladly oblige, I suggest you simply relax.'

'Oh, go to hell!' she was stung into retorting as he reached out and switched off the bedside lamp.

Seconds later Alyse was aware of his warm breath against her temple, and she lay perfectly still, willing the nervous tautness in her body to ease, then slowly her eyelids flickered down as sheer exhaustion gradually took its toll and sleep provided blissful oblivion.

CHAPTER EIGHT

THE ensuing few days provided an opportunity for Alyse to become better acquainted with Rachel, for each morning Aleksi's stepmother arrived in time to help with Georg's bath, then they would each take it in turns to feed him his bottle before settling him back into his cot.

There was time for a leisurely morning tea and a chat before eating a light midday lunch, after which Georg was fed, resettled, and placed into Melanie's care for the afternoon while they explored one of the many shopping complexes scattered along the Gold Coast's tourist strip.

Alexandros joined his son in a daily round of building site inspections, meetings and consultations, from which they returned together each evening.

Dinner was inevitably an informal meal, with both women sharing the preparation, and Alyse felt faintly envious of the friendship Aleksi shared with his parents. It was genuine and uncontrived, and while part of her enjoyed sharing their company, another constantly warned against forming too close an attachment for two people who, after her intended separation and divorce from Aleksi, would no longer find it possible to regard her with any affection. Somehow such a thought caused her immeasurable pain.

The nights were something else, for in Aleksi's arms she became increasingly uninhibited, to such an extent that she began to hate her own traitorous body almost as much as she assured herself that she hated *him*.

Arrangements for the party Aleksi insisted they host to celebrate their marriage proved remarkably simple, with a series of telephone calls to a variety of guests, and the hiring of a reputable catering firm.

All that remained for Alyse to do was to arrange for Melanie to babysit, and select something suitable to wear.

While the former was remarkably simple, choosing a dress took considerable time and care, although Rachel's wholehearted approval proved invaluable, and the silk and lace ensemble in deep cream highlighted the texture of her skin and the brilliant sapphire-blue of her eyes. The bodice was demure with elbow-length sleeves, with a fitted waist that accentuated her small waist, and the skirt fell in graceful folds to a fashionable length.

The guests were due to begin arriving at eight, and Alyse settled Georg upstairs just after six, then she hastily showered, taking extreme care with her hair and make-up.

Nerves were hell and damnation, she decided silently, cursing softly at the unsteadiness of her hand, and she cleansed her eyelids and started all over again.

She wished fervently that the evening were over and done with. Aleksi's friends would be super-critical of his new wife, and she had little doubt she would be dissected piece by piece from the top of her head to the tips of her elegant designer shoes.

An hour later she stood back from the mirror and viewed her overall appearance with a tiny frown.

'Problems?'

She turned at once at the sound of that deep drawling voice, noting that Aleksi displayed an inherent sophistication attired in a dark suit, white shirt and sombre tie, and she envied him the air of relaxed calm he was able to exude without any seeming effort at all.

Her eyes clouded with anxiety. 'What do you think?'

He took his time answering, and she suffered his slow appraisal with increasing apprehension.

'Beautiful,' he told her, lifting a hand to tilt her chin fractionally. His smile held a mesmerising quality, and she ran the tip of her tongue along the edge of her lower lip in a gesture of nervousness. 'I'm almost sorry I have to share you with a room full of people.' His eyes gleamed darkly. 'An intimate evening *à deux* would be more appropriate.'

Her lashes swept up in a deliberate attempt at guile. 'And waste this dress? It cost a fortune.'

His mouth curved with humour. 'I'm impressed, believe me.' Releasing her chin, he caught hold of her hand. 'Melanie is already upstairs with Georg and an enviable collection of law books. Rachel and Alexandros have arrived. The caterers have everything under control, and there's time for a quiet drink before the first of our guests are due to arrive.'

Alyse wondered if it was too late to opt out, and some of her indecision must have been apparent in her expression, for he bent forward and brushed his lips against her temple.

'It's no big deal, Alyse. In any case, I'll be here.'

'Maybe that's what I'm afraid of,' she said with undue solemnity, and saw his smile widen with sardonic cynicism.

'Ah, this is the Alyse I know best.'

Suddenly flip, she responded, 'I wasn't aware there was more than one of me.'

His husky laughter brought a soft tinge of colour to her cheeks, and she made no demure as he led the way out into the lounge.

Everything appeared superb, Alyse decided a few hours later as she drifted politely from one group of guests to another. Background music filtered through a sophisticated electronic system, and hired staff circulated among the guests with professional ease, proffering trays of tastefully prepared morsels of food. Champagne flowed from a seemingly inexhaustible supply, and she had been introduced to so many people it was impossible to remember more than a few of their names. Beautiful, elegantly attired women, who seemed discreetly intent on discovering the latest in social gossip, while the man stood in segregated groups talking business—primarily their own as related to the state of the country's current economy.

'Darling, you really *must* come along,' a gorgeous blonde insisted, and Alyse brought her attention back to the small group of women who had commandeered her attention. 'It's a worthwhile charity. The models are superb and the clothes will be absolutely stunning.' Perfect white teeth gleamed between equally perfectly painted red lips, and the smile portrayed practised sincerity. 'Annabel will be there, Chrissie, Kate, and Marta. You'll sit with us, of course.'

'Can I let you know?' Alyse managed politely, and saw the ice-blue eyes narrow fractionally.

'Of course. Aleksi has my number.'

Within seconds she was alone again, but not for long.

'Do you need rescuing?'

A warm smile curved the edges of her mouth at the welcome intrusion of her mother-in-law. 'How did you guess?'

'Everything is going beautifully, my dear,' Rachel complimented. 'You're doing very well,' she added gently, and Alyse sobered slightly, although her smile didn't falter for a second.

'I'm the cynosure of all eyes. Circumspectly assessed, analysed, and neatly categorised—rather like a prize piece of merchandise. Will I pass muster, do you think?'

'With flying colours,' Rachel told her, and Alyse could have genuinely hugged her.

'Ah, an ally,' she breathed gratefully. 'It seems I should join numerous committees, play the requisite twice weekly game of tennis, frequent daily aerobic workouts, attend weekly classes in exotic flower arrangement, and become part of a circle who gather for social luncheons.' A wicked gleam lit her expressive eyes. 'What hours left free in the day are advisably spent visiting a beauty salon, shopping, or, importantly, organising the next luncheon, dinner party, or simply the informal get-together for Sunday brunch.'

'You don't aspire to joining the society treadmill?'

'Not to any great extent.' Her shoulders lifted slightly in an elegant shrug. 'A few luncheons might be fun. A stunning blonde whose name escapes me issued an invitation to a fashion parade held at Sanctuary Cove on Tuesday. Perhaps we could go together?'

'Lovely,' the older woman enthused. 'It will give Alexandros an opportunity to spend a day on the golf course.'

Alyse let her gaze wander round the large room, noting idly that the various guests gave every appearance of enjoying themselves. Although who wouldn't, she thought wryly, when provided with fine food and wine, and glittering company? The women dripped diamonds, and several wore mink, elegantly styled jackets slung with apparent carelessness over slim designer-clad shoulders.

'Do you know many of the people here?' she queried tentatively.

'Most of the men are business associates, with their various wives or girlfriends,' Rachel revealed with a sympathetic smile. 'The glamorous blonde who last engaged you in conversation is Serita Hubbard—her husband is a very successful property speculator. The brunette talking to Serita is Kate, the daughter of one of Aleksi's best friends—that's Paul, her father, deep in conversation with Aleksi and Alexandros.' Rachel paused, tactfully drawing Alyse's attention to a stunning couple on the far side of the room. 'Dominic Rochas, and his sister Solange. Together they represent a highly reputable firm of interior designers.'

Tall, slim and beautifully dressed, they could easily have passed as models for an exclusive fashion house, Alyse decided without envy. Somehow they didn't seem real, and instead were merely players portraying an expected part on the stage of life.

'Given time, I'm sure I'll get to know them all,' she ventured quietly.

'Aleksi and Georg are very fortunate to have you,' Rachel complimented softly.

With a hand that shook slightly Alyse picked up her glass and savoured its contents in the hope that the excellent champagne would calm her nerves. It was all too apparent that Rachel held fond hopes for the apparent affection between her stepson and his new bride to blossom and eventually bloom into love.

Something that Aleksi seemed to deliberately foster by ensuring his glance lingered a few seconds too long, augmenting it with the touch of his hand on her arm, at her waist, not to mention the lazy indulgence he accorded her on numerous occasions in the presence of his parents.

'Put several business friends together in the same room,' a familiar voice drawled at her elbow, 'and inevitably the conversation drifts away from social pleasantries.'

Talk of the devil! Alyse turned her head slowly towards Aleksi and gave him a brilliant smile. 'I hardly noticed your absence.'

'I think that could be termed an indirect admonition,' Alexandros declared with humour as he directed his wife a musing glance. 'Yes?'

'Alyse and I have been enjoying each other's company,' Rachel acknowledged with considerable diplomacy.

'Aleksi *darling*!' an incredibly warm voice gushed with the barest hint of an accent. 'We're impossibly late, but Tony got held up in Brisbane, and we simply *flew* down. Say you forgive us?'

Alyse sensed the effervescent laughter threatening to burst out from the large-framed woman whose entire bearing could only be described as *majestic*. A dark purple silk trouser-suit with voluminous matching knee-length jacket, long trailing scarves and an abundance of jewellery completed an ensemble that on anyone else would have looked ludicrous.

'Siobhan!' Aleksi's smile was genuinely warm as he accepted her embrace. 'Tony. Allow me to introduce my wife, Alyse.'

Alyse immediately became the focus of two pairs of eyes, one set of which was femininely shrewd yet totally lacking in calculation.

'She looks perfect, darling,' Siobhan pronounced softly, and Alyse had the uncanny feeling she had been subjected to some kind of test and had unwittingly passed. 'Is she?'

Aleksi's eyes gleamed with silent humour. 'Incredibly so.'

'Siobhan, you're outrageous,' her husband drawled in resignation. 'I imagine the poor girl is almost witless with nerves.'

Wonderfully warm dark eyes gleamed as they held hers. 'Are you?' asked Siobhan.

'Like a lamb in a den of lions,' Alyse admitted with a wry smile.

Mellifluous laughter flowed richly from Siobhan's throat. 'Several of the female gender present undoubtedly are, my dear. Especially where your gorgeous hunk of a husband is concerned.'

'I suppose there must be a certain fascination for his dark brooding charm,' Alyse considered with a devilish gleam, and Siobhan grinned, totally unabashed.

'He's a sexy beast, darling. To some, it's almost a fatal attraction.'

Alyse merely smiled, and Siobhan said softly, 'How delightful—you're shy!'

'A fascinating quality,' Aleksi agreed, taking hold of Alyse's hand and threading his fingers through her own.

She tried to tug her hand away, and felt his fingers tighten in silent warning. 'Perhaps we could get together for dinner soon? Now, if you'll excuse us, we really must circulate. Enjoy yourselves,' he bade genially.

It was impossible to protest, and Alyse allowed Aleksi to lead her from one group to another in the large room, pausing for five minutes, sometimes ten, as they engaged in conversation. Georg's existence had precipitated a marriage that had aroused speculative conjecture, and by the time they had come full circle her facial muscles felt tight from maintaining a constant smile, and her nerves were raw beneath an abundance of thinly veiled curiosity.

'Another drink?' asked Aleksi.

Dared she? Somehow it seemed essential to appear to be in total command, and she had merely picked a few morsels from each course during dinner and barely nibbled from the abundance of food constantly offered by hired staff throughout the evening. 'I'd love some coffee.'

An eyebrow slanted in quizzical query. 'I can't tempt you with champagne-spiked orange juice?' His gaze was direct and vaguely analytical, and Alyse was unable to suppress the faint quickening of her pulse.

He had the strangest effect on her equilibrium, making her aware of a primitive alchemy, a dramatic pull of the senses almost beyond her comprehension, for it didn't seem possible to be able to physically enjoy sex with someone she actively disliked. Hated, she amended, unwilling to accord him much favour. Yet he projected an enviable aura of power, a distinctive mesh of male charisma and sensuality that alerted the interest of women—a primeval recognition that made her feel uncommonly resentful.

'I'd prefer coffee,' she responded with forced lightness, and he laughed, a deep, husky sound that sent shivers scudding down the length of her spine.

'The need for a clear head?' His teeth gleamed white for an instant, then became hidden beneath the curve of his mouth.

'Yes,' she admitted without prevarication.

'Stay here, and I'll fetch some.'

'I'd rather come with you.'

He examined her features, assessing the bright eyes and pale cheeks with daunting scrutiny. 'No one here would dare harm so much as a hair on your beautiful head,' he alluded cynically.

'Forgive me if I don't believe you.' She hadn't meant to sound bitter, but the implication was there, and she felt immeasurably angry—with herself, for allowing him to catch a glimpse of her vulnerability.

Without a further word he led her towards a table where an attractively attired waitress was dispensing tea and coffee, and within seconds he had placed a cup between her nerveless fingers, watching as she sipped the hot aromatic brew appreciatively while her eyes skimmed the room.

'When you've finished, we'll dance,' he told her.

Alyse brought her gaze back to the indomitable man at her side. 'You've succeeded admirably at playing the perfect husband all evening. Dancing cheek-to-cheek might be overdoing it, don't you think?'

His eyes were dark and unfathomable. 'Inconceivable, of course, that I might want to?'

She suddenly felt as if she'd skated on to very thin ice, and she resorted to restrained anger in defence. 'I'm damned if I'll act out a charade!'

'Are you so sure it will be?'

This was an infinitely dangerous game, and she wasn't at all sure she wanted to play. Yet in a room full of people, what else could she do but comply?

Her eyes glittered as he removed the empty cup from her hand and put it down on the nearby table, and her smile was deliberately winsome as he drew her out on to the terrace and into his arms.

There were strategically placed lights casting a muted glow over landscaped gardens, and the air was fresh and cool.

'You have a large number of friends,' Alyse remarked in a desperate bid to break the silence.

'Business associates, acquaintances with whom I maintain social contact,' Aleksi corrected wryly.

She tilted her head slightly. 'How cynical!'

'You think so?'

He was amused, damn him! *'Yes.'*

'Careful, little cat,' he cautioned softly, controlling with ease her effort to put some distance between them. 'Your claws are showing.'

'If they are, it's because I detest what you're doing.'

'Dancing with my wife?'

'Oh, stop being so damned—*impossible*! You know very well what I mean.'

'This party was arranged specifically to give a number of important people the opportunity to meet you. The reason for our marriage is none of their business.'

'There are several women present who appear to think it is!'

'Their problem, not mine.' He sounded so clinical, so damned—detached, that she felt sickened.

'Let me go. I want to check on Georg.'

'Melanie is ensconced upstairs doing precisely that,' drawled Aleksi, refusing to relinquish his hold. 'In a minute we'll go back inside and mingle with our guests.'

'I hate you!'

'At least it's a healthy emotion.'

It didn't *feel* healthy! In fact, it razed her nerves and turned her into a seething ball of fury.

For what remained of the evening Alyse displayed the expected role of hostess with charm and dignity, so much so that she surely deserved a medal for perseverance, she decided as she stood at her

husband's side and said goodbye to the last remaining clutch of guests.

Only when the tail-lights of the final car dis-
appeared from sight and Aleksi had firmly closed
the front door did she allow the mask to slip.

'I'll pay the babysitter, and activate Georg's electronic monitor,' Aleksi determined. 'There's no
point in disturbing him simply to move him
downstairs.'

The fact that he was right didn't preclude her
need to oppose him, and she opened her mouth,
only to close it again beneath the force of his
forefinger.

'Don't argue.'

She drew back her head as if touched by flame,
and her eyes flashed with anger. 'I'll do as I damn
well please!'

His expression assumed a musing indolence. 'Go
to bed.'

She was so angry, it almost consumed her. 'And
wait dutifully for you to join me?'

Without a word he turned and made for the
stairs, and she watched his ascent with impotent
rage.

Damned if she'd obey and retire meekly to the
bedroom! Although at several minutes past two in
the morning it hardly made sense to think of anything else. And perversity, simply for the sheer hell
of it, was infinitely unwise.

Except she didn't feel like taking a sensible
course, and without pausing to give her actions
further thought she crossed the lounge and made
her way downstairs.

The caterers had been extremely efficient, for apart from a few glasses there was little evidence that a party had taken place.

A quick vacuum of the carpets and the room would be restored to its usual immaculate state, she decided, and, uncaring of the late hour, she retrieved the necessary cleaner and set it in motion.

She had almost finished when the motor came to a sudden stop, and she turned to see Aleksi standing a few feet distant with the disconnected cord held in his hand.

'This can surely wait?' His voice was deceptively mild, and didn't fool her in the slightest.

'It will only take another minute, then it's done.'

'In the morning, Alyse.'

'I'd prefer to do it now.' It was as if she was on a rollercoaster to self-destruction, able to see her ultimate destination yet powerless to stop.

'Obstinacy simply for the sheer hell of it is foolish, don't you think?' Aleksi queried, depressing the automatic cord rewind button, and Alyse glared at him balefully.

'Aren't you being equally stubborn?' she returned at once.

He spared the elegant gold watch at his wrist a cursory glance. 'Two-thirty in the morning isn't conducive to a definitive discussion.'

'So once again I must play the part of a subjugated wife!'

His eyes narrowed, assuming a daunting hardness that was at variance with the softness of his voice. 'Perhaps you'd care to clarify that remark?'

Alyse stood defiant. 'I don't like being continually dictated to,' she told him angrily. 'And I especially don't like being taken for granted.' She lifted a hand, then let it fall down to her side. 'I feel like a child, forced to conform. And I'm not,' she insisted, helpless in the face of her own anger.

'Aren't you?' Aleksi brushed his fingers across her heated cheeks. 'Most women would exult in my wealth and scheme to acquire all life's so-called luxuries.'

'Are you condemning me as a child because I'm unwilling to play the vamp in bed?'

'What a delightfully evocative phrase!'

'I hate you, do you understand? *Hate* you,' she said fiercely, then gave a startled cry as he calmly took hold of her arms and lifted her over his shoulder. 'What do you think you're doing?'

He turned and began walking towards the stairs. 'I would have thought it was obvious.'

'Put me down, damn you!' There was a terrible sense of indignity at being carried in such a manner, and she hit out at him, clenching her hands into fists as she railed them against his back. 'Bastard!' she accused as he reached the ground floor and crossed the lounge. *'Barbarian!'*

On entering their bedroom he pulled her down to stand facing him, and she looked at him through a mist of anger.

'This seems to be the only level on which we effectively communicate.' His eyes were hard and inflexible.

'Speak for yourself!' she flung incautiously.

His eyes lanced hers, their expression dark and forbidding. 'I'm tempted to make you beg for my possession.'

'What's stopping you?'

'Little fool,' Aleksi condemned with dangerous silkiness. 'Aren't you in the least afraid of my temper?'

'What would you do? Beat me?'

'Maybe I should, simply to teach you the lesson you deserve.'

'And what about the lesson I consider *you* deserve?' cried Alyse, tried almost beyond endurance. 'For forcing me into marriage, your bed...' She faltered to a shaky halt, hating him more than she thought it was possible to hate anyone.

'Your love for Antonia and Georg surpassed any minor considerations.'

'*Minor!*' An entire flood of words threatened to spill from her, except that his mouth covered hers with brutal possession, effectively stilling the flow.

'You don't hate me as much as you pretend,' Aleksi drawled as he lifted his head, and she flung heatedly,

'There's no pretence whatsoever in the way I feel about you!'

Placing a thumb and forefinger beneath her chin, he lifted it so that she had no option but to look at him.

'Perhaps you should query whether a proportion of anger doesn't originate with yourself for enjoying something you insist is merely physical lust,' he alluded silkily.

Did he know how impossible it was for her to come to terms with her own traitorous body? Even now, part of her wanted to melt into his arms, while another part urged her to pull away. It was crazy to feel like this, to be prey to a gamut of emotions so complex that understanding why seemed beyond comprehension.

'I don't enjoy it!' To admit, even to herself, that she did, was something she refused to concede.

'No?'

Aleksi sounded indolently amused, and she flinched away from the brush of his fingers as he trailed them along the edge of her jaw, then traced the throbbing cord at her neck before exploring the hollows at the base of her throat.

'Such a sweet mouth,' he mocked gently, lowering his own to within inches of her softly curved lips. 'And so very kissable.'

The breath seemed to catch in her throat. 'Stop it.' Her eyes clung to his, bright, angry, yet intensely vulnerable. 'Please.'

'Why?' Aleksi murmured as he touched the tip of his tongue against the sensual centre of her lower lip, then began to edge gently inwards in an evocative discovery of the sensitive moist tissues.

'Aleksi.' His name whispered from her lips with something akin to despair. 'No!'

A hand slid beneath her hair, cupping her nape, while the other slipped to her lower back, urging her close, and his mouth continued its light tasting; teasing, deliberately withholding the promise of passion until his touch became an exquisite torture.

She ached for him to deepen the kiss, and she gave a faint sigh as his mouth hardened in irrefutable possession, wiping out every vestige of conscious thought. A deep flame flared into pulsating life beneath his sensual mastery, and each separate nerve-end tingled alive with unbridled ardency as she gave the response he sought.

His clothes, hers, were a dispensable barrier, and she made no protest as he set about freeing them both of any material restriction.

Her body arched of its own accord as his mouth trailed her collarbone and began a downward movement to her breast, silently inviting the wicked ecstasy of his erotic touch, and she cried out as he caressed the delicate swelling bud, luxuriating in the waves of sensation pulsing through her body.

A faint cry of protest silvered the night air as he shifted slightly, then she gave a husky purr of pleasure as he trailed the valley to render a similar supplication to its aching twin.

With consummate skill his fingers traced an evocative path over her silky skin, playing each sensitive pleasure-spot to fever-pitch until she was filled with a deep, aching need that only physical release could assuage.

Alyse barely registered the silken sheets beneath her back, yet the relief she craved was withheld as his mouth feathered the path of his hand in a sensual tasting that was impossibly erotic, making the blood sing through her veins like wildfire until her very soul seemed *his*, and she began to plead, tiny guttural sounds that her conscious mind registered but refused to accept as remotely *hers*.

Hardly aware of her actions, she reached for his head, her fingers curling into the thickness of his hair as she attempted to divert his attention, wanting, *needing* to feel his mouth on hers in hard, hungry passion.

Like something wild and untamed, her body began to thresh beneath his in blatant invitation until at last he plunged deep into the silken core, creating a pulsating rhythmic pattern that took her to the heights and beyond in an explosion of sensual ecstasy that was undeniably his pleasure as well as her own.

For a long time afterwards she seemed encased in a hazy rosy glow, and as she drifted slowly back to reality she became aware of the featherlight touch of his fingers as they traced the moist contours of her body.

She didn't feel capable of moving, and a tiny bubble of laughter died in her throat scarcely before it began.

'What do you find so amusing?'

Alyse turned her head slowly to meet the deep slumbering passion still lurking in those gleaming eyes so close to her own. 'I think you'd better stop. There's a young baby upstairs who'll soon wake for his early morning bottle.'

Aleksi's lips curved warmly as he lifted a hand to her hair and tucked a few collective tendrils back behind her ear. 'I'll feed him, then come back to bed.'

She tried to inject a degree of condemnation into her voice, and failed miserably. 'You're insatiable!'

His lips touched her shoulder, then slid to the curve of her neck in an evocative caress. 'So, my sweet, are you.'

Remembering just how she had reacted in his arms brought a tide of telltale colour to her cheeks, and her eyes clouded with shame.

'Don't,' he bade softly, 'be embarrassed at losing yourself so completely in the sexual act.'

'I might have been faking,' she said unsteadily, and almost died at the degree of lazy humour evident in the gleaming eyes so close to her own.

'Liar,' he drawled. 'Your delight was totally spontaneous.'

'And you're the expert.' She hadn't meant to sound bitter, but it tinged her voice none the less, and her lashes descended to form a protective veil against his compelling scrutiny.

'Sufficiently experienced to give consideration to your pleasure as well as my own.'

'For that I should be grateful?'

'I would advise you against provoking me to demonstrate the difference.'

A faint chill feathered across the surface of her skin, and she shivered. 'I'm going to have a shower.'

She half expected him to stop her, and when he didn't she felt vaguely resentful, electing to take over-long beneath the warm jet of water and even longer attending to her toilette.

Emerging into the bedroom, she slipped carefully into bed and lay still, only to realise within seconds that Aleksi was already asleep, his breathing steady and uncontrived.

For several long minutes she studied his features, aware that even in repose there was an inherent strength apparent, a force that was slightly daunting. Relaxed, his mouth assumed a firm curve, and she experienced the almost irresistible desire to touch it with her own.

Are you *mad*? an inner voice taunted.

With a hand that shook slightly Alyse reached out and snapped off the bedside lamp, then laid her head on the pillow, allowing innate weariness to transport her into a deep, dreamless sleep.

CHAPTER NINE

SUNDAY showed promise of becoming one of those beautiful sunny days south-east Queensland was renowned for producing in the midst of a tropical winter. A slight breeze barely stirred the air, and the sea was a clear translucent blue with scarcely a ripple to disturb its surface.

'The weather is too good not to take the boat out,' Aleksi declared as Alyse entered the kitchen after bathing and feeding Georg. She smelled of baby talc, and her eyes were still soft with the sheer delight of his existence.

Crossing to the pantry, she extracted muesli, retrieved milk from the fridge, then poured generous portions of both into a bowl and carried it to the table.

'I'm sure Rachel and Alexandros will enjoy a day out on the Bay,' she said with studied politeness, and incurred Aleksi's sharp scrutiny.

'There can be no doubt you will come too.'

She forced herself to look at him carefully, noting the almost indecently broad shoulders, the firm sculptured features that portrayed inherent strength of will. He had finished his breakfast, and was seated opposite, a half-finished cup of coffee within easy reach.

'I'm not sure it's fair to expect Melanie to come at such short notice, especially on a Sunday, and particularly when she babysat Georg last night.' Her gaze was remarkably level as she held his dark, faintly brooding gaze. 'Besides, I don't think Georg should be left too often in a babysitter's care. Young children need constancy in their lives, not a succession of minders their parents install merely as a delegation of responsibility to ensure the pursuit of their social existence.'

One eyebrow rose to form a cynical arch. 'My dear Alyse, I totally agree. However, Georg is so young, his major concern is being kept clean and dry, with sustenance available whenever he needs it. I doubt if being left in Melanie's care will damage his psyche. Besides, we'll be back before five.'

Her eyes grew stormy. 'Are you always so damnably persistent?'

'My parents like you,' drawled Aleksi. 'And I'm prepared to do anything that's in my power to please them during the length of their stay.'

'With that in mind,' she began heatedly, 'I would have thought they'd both want to spend as much time with their grandson as possible. Not socialise, or sail the high seas.'

He was silent for a few long minutes, then he said silkily. 'During the past year they've seen their son horrifically injured, and suffered the despair of knowing his life-span was severely limited. As soon as his condition stabilised, Rachel and Alexandros turned their home into a veritable clinic, hiring a team of highly qualified medical staff to care for Georgiou. They gave up everything to spend time with him, taking alternate shifts along with the staff so that either one was always at his side.' He paused, and his voice hardened slightly. 'Now they need to relax and begin to enjoy life again. If that entails socialising and sailing, then so be it.' His eyes assumed an inexorable bleakness. 'Have I made myself clear?'

Alyse pushed her bowl aside, her appetite gone. 'Painfully so.'

'Eat your breakfast.'

'I no longer feel hungry.'

'Maybe my absence will help it return,' Aleksi said drily as he rose to his feet. 'I'll be in the study, making a few calls.'

Within two hours they were on board a large lux-uriously-fitted cruiser that lay moored to a jetty on the canal at the bottom of Aleksi's garden.

Alyse had elected to wear tailored white cotton trousers with a yellow sweater. Rachel was simi-larly attired, and both men wore jeans and casual dark sweaters.

'This is heaven!' Rachel breathed, turning towards her stepson.

Alyse almost gasped out loud at the warmth of his smile as it rested on Rachel's features.

'We'll berth at Sanctuary Cove for lunch. After-wards, you and Alyse can wander among the bou-tiques while Alexandros and I sit lazily in the sun enjoying a beer.'

'You're spoiling her,' Alexandros chided his son in a teasing accented drawl, and Rachel laughed.

'All women adore being spoiled by men, don't they, Alyse?'

She was doomed no matter what she said, and, summoning a brilliant smile, she ventured sweetly. 'Definitely.'

Aleksi shot his father a mocking glance. 'I have a feeling the Cove could prove an expensive stopover.'

After a superb seafood lunch the two women strolled at will, visiting several exclusive shops where they purchased a variety of casual resort-styled ensembles, and Alyse fell in love with a pair of imported shoes which she recklessly added to a collection of brightly designed plastic carrier-bags already in her possession.

'What did I tell you?' drawled Aleksi with amusement as Alyse and Rachel joined them in the Yacht Club's lounge.

'Alyse had bought the most gorgeous outfit,' Rachel enthused, taking hold of her husband's outstretched hand, and her sparkling smile softened as he lifted it to his lips in a gesture that made Alyse's heart execute an unaccustomed flip in silent acknowledgment of the love these two people shared. 'I've persuaded her to wear it to the fashion parade Serita Hubbard invited us to attend at the Cove on Tuesday.'

The cruiser traversed the Bay to reach Sovereign Islands just before five, and after relieving Melanie Alyse checked on Georg to find him stirring and almost ready for his bottle.

'Let me,' Rachel offered at his first wakening cry. 'I'm sure you'll want to shower and change.'

'Thanks,' Alyse acquiesced in gratitude. 'I won't be long.'

When she returned, Aleksi and Alexandros were in the kitchen, and Georg was seated on Rachel's knee, his eyes moving from one to the other, his tiny fists beating the air in undisguised delight.

'See?' beamed Alexandros with Greek pride. 'He is strong, this little one. Look at those legs, those hands! He will grow tall.' He shot his son a laughing glance. 'A good protector for his sisters, an example for his brothers. Yes?'

It was difficult for Alyse to keep her smile in place, but she managed it—just. Part of her wanted to cry out that brothers or sisters for Georgiou's son didn't form part of her plan. Yet she could hardly blame Alexandros for assuming his son's marriage would include other children in years to come.

And what of Aleksi? Was he content with a marriage of expediency which provided a woman in his bed and a mother for his children? Or would he eventually become bored and seek sexual gratification elsewhere?

Far better that she steel her heart against any emotional involvement. Two years wasn't a lifetime, and afterwards she could rebuild her future. A future for herself, for Georg.

Dinner was an impromptu meal of grilled steak and an assortment of salads, with fresh fruit, and followed by a leisurely coffee in the lounge.

Rachel and Alexandros took their leave at nine, declaring a need for an early night, and Alyse felt strangely tired herself from the combination of sea air and warm winter sunshine.

'I'll tidy the kitchen,' she declared as Aleksi closed the front door and set the security system. 'We'll do it together.'

She was already walking ahead of him. 'I can manage.' For some reason his presence swamped her, and she wanted to be alone.

There were only a few cups and saucers, glasses the men had used for a liqueur, and she quickly rinsed and stacked them in the dishwasher, all too aware of Aleksi's presence.

'All finished,' she announced, and made to step past him.

'I've opened a separate bank account with a balance sufficient to meet whatever cash you need,' he told her. 'The details are in the escritoire in your sitting-room, as well as a supplementary card accessing my charge account.'

Alyse felt a surge of resentment, and forced herself to take a deep calming breath. 'I'd prefer to use my own money, and I already have a charge account.'

His gaze focused on her features, noting the faint wariness in the set of her mouth, the proud tilt of her chin, and the determination apparent in those beautiful blue eyes. 'Why be so fiercely independent? It's surely a husband's right to support his wife?'

'The housekeeping, and anything Georg needs,' she agreed. 'But I'll pay for my own clothes.'

'And if I insist?'

'You can insist as much as you like,' she retaliated. 'I won't be cowed into submissive obedience simply out of deference to a marriage certificate.'

Aleksi's eyes hardened fractionally, and his mouth curved to form a mocking smile. 'An enlightened feminist?'

Now she was really angry! 'If you wanted a decorative doll whose sole pleasure was to acquire jewellery and designer clothes at your expense, then you made a mistake in choosing me!'

'I don't think so,' he drawled.

'You *enjoy* our parody of a marriage?' she demanded, and was incensed to hear his husky laughter.

Lifting a hand, he slid it beneath the curtain of her hair, threading his fingers to tug gently at its length, tilting her head.

'I enjoy *you*,' Aleksi accorded silkily. 'The way you continually oppose me, simply for the sheer hell of it.'

Alyse forced herself to hold his gaze, although she was unable to prevent the slight trembling movement of her lips, and she glimpsed the faint flaring evident in the depths of his eyes.

'Be warned, it's a fight you may not win.'

She wanted to lash out and hit him, and only the chill sense of purpose apparent in those dark features stopped her. 'Do you imagine I'll be swayed into becoming emotionally involved simply because you can——' She faltered, momentarily lost for words in the heat of her anger.

'Turn you on?'

'Oh!' she raged, gasping out loud as he drew her close against him, and her struggles were in vain as his head lowered to hers. His lips were firm and warm, caressing with evocative slowness, and she wanted to cry out against his flagrant seduction. It would be so easy to close her eyes and allow herself to be swept away by the magic of his lovemaking. Against her will, the blood began to sing in her veins and her bones turned to liquid as sheer sensation overtook sanity. She became lost, adrift without sense of direction until anger at her own treacherous emotions rose to the surface, and she forcibly broke free from his devastating mouth.

'Let me go, damn you,' she said shakily, straining against the strength of his arms, and her eyes were clouded with an inner struggle she had no intention of confessing—even to herself.

Aleksi held her effortlessly, his expression an inscrutable mask, and it seemed an age before he spoke.

'Go to bed. I have to go over some plans due to be submitted at a meeting tomorrow morning.'

Without a word she turned and moved away from him, her breathing becoming more ragged with every single step, and by the time she reached the bedroom she felt as if she'd run a mile.

Perversity demanded that she sleep in the adjoining sitting-room, but at the last moment common sense prevailed.

What was the point? she decided wearily as she slid in between the sheets on her side of the large bed. Aleksi would undoubtedly remove her, and she was too tired tonight to fight.

An hour later she was still awake, a victim of her own vivid imagination, and it seemed an age before she heard the soft almost imperceptible sound of his entry into the bedroom. In the reflected illumination of Georg's night-light she watched through lowered lashes as he discarded his clothes, and she unconsciously held her breath as he slid into bed. Minutes later she heard his breathing slow and assume a deep steady rhythm.

He had fallen asleep! For some unknown reason that angered her unbearably, and she cursed her own feminine contrariness for the slow-burning ache that gradually consumed her body until she was aflame with the need for physical assuagement.

Alyse glanced around the high-domed marquee with seeming interest. There were more than a hundred women present, each so elegantly attired she could only conclude that their main purpose was to catch the photographer's eye and thereby make the society pages.

Her vivid peacock-green silk suit teamed with black accessories was an attractive foil for Rachel's ensemble in cream and gold.

Champagne flowed, pressed eagerly upon them by handsome formally suited young men.

'Have they been hired by an agency especially for the occasion, do you think?' Alyse queried quietly of Rachel.

'Definitely. They're too much in awe of the cream of society's glitterati.'

'And hopeful of making a conquest?'

Rachel cast her a faintly wicked smile. 'Don't look round, but you've definitely caught one young man's eye.'

Alyse gave a negligent shrug in silent uninterest, and sipped at her champagne. 'Tell me about Greece. Do you like living there?'

Rachel's expression softened. 'We have several homes in various parts of the world. Some are splendid, but the one I love best is situated in the bay of a small island off the main coast. It's a fairy-tale—no cars, just peace and solitude with the only means of entry via boat or helicopter. It was there that Alexandros and Aleksi taught Georgiou to sail.'

Alyse sensed the older woman's sadness, and touched her hand in a gesture of silent sympathy.

'It's all right, my dear. As one gets older, one realises there is only *now*. Memories can't be changed, and I count myself fortunate that mine are many and such happy ones. Our two sons were a constant delight, although Georgiou was the friv-olous one, coveting the thrill of the moment behind the wheel of a high-powered motorboat or car. I lived in constant fear of the day he might make a misjudgment.'

Alyse had to ask. 'And Aleksi?'

'He was more serious, and despite the difference in age and character he and Georgiou were very close. During those awful months after the ac-cident, he flew back and forth to Athens countless times, and when he wasn't there he rang every second day.'

'Alyse! How wonderful of you to bring Rachel, darling,' a husky feminine voice enthused, and she turned her head to see Serita Hubbard in a vivid white ensemble that undoubtedly bore a Diane Fries label.

'Serita,' she returned politely.

'I've arranged for us to be seated together at lunch. If we do become separated during the fashion parade, just meet me in front of the marquee afterwards.' Serita's smile flashed friendly warmth. 'Must dash, there's a slight muddle with tickets supposed to be handed out by one of the committee members. She thought I'd collected them, and I was under the impression that *she* had. I need to show my list to the organiser. There are quite a few people here you've met, and Solange said she'd probably be running late. Do mingle, won't you?'

It was a brilliantly orchestrated parade, quite the best Alyse had attended, for the models were top-class professionals and the clothes not only superb, but many were available from the Cove boutiques.

'See anything you particularly like?' Rachel asked, then laughed as she glimpsed the appreciative gleam in her daughter-in-law's eyes.

'An hour with our marked catalogues after lunch?' Alyse suggested.

'Definitely,' Rachel agreed. 'And talking of lunch, we'd better head for the marquee entrance.'

The restaurant chosen for the venue was cantilevered out over the water, with splendid views of the harbour-front villas and a flotilla of luxury craft moored at an adjacent marina.

Solange was seated opposite, beside Serita, Marta, Chrissie, Kate and Annabel, and Alyse felt as if she was facing an inquisition committee.

The same impeccably suited young men who had so earnestly served champagne before the parade also waited on tables, and Alyse found it amusing to be the recipient of one particular man's attentive solicitude.

'Darling, you do seem to have made a hit,' Solange declared artlessly. 'Are you going to slip him your phone number?'

Without faltering, Alyse responded with an absence of guile. 'With a young baby to care for, I haven't the time or the inclination to foster the attention of a toy-boy.' She offered a brilliant smile. 'Besides, I doubt if Aleksi would be amused.'

Solange's eyes narrowed slightly. 'A little jealousy stimulates a marriage, surely?'

Oh, heavens, she was beginning to feel like a butterfly pinned to the wall, with numerous pairs of interested eyes waiting to see if she'd squirm! 'Do you think so?' she queried, then gave a light faintly husky laugh. 'Aleksi would probably beat me.'

Serita smiled in silent amusement, while Solange merely fixed Alyse with an unblinking glare. 'Dominic insists we host a dinner party on Saturday evening,' she drawled. 'I'll ring Aleksi with the details.' Her gaze rested on Rachel. 'You must come too, of course.'

'We leave for Sydney tomorrow to spend time with my sister, so we won't be here, I'm afraid,' Rachel declined graciously, and Solange gave a slight negligent shrug.

It was after two when Alyse and Rachel managed to slip away, and within an hour and a half they were heading towards Sovereign Islands with a few selected purchases reposing on the rear seat of the car.

Alyse had planned an informal dinner at home for Rachel and Alexandros's last evening on the Coast, and there was a certain sense of sadness apparent when it came time for them to leave, for she would miss Rachel's company.

'A week isn't long,' the older woman assured her as she gave her an affectionate hug. 'And I'll phone frequently to check on my grandson.'

'I shall probably have to restrain her from making at least three calls a day,' Alexandros declared with amusement as he slid into the rear seat of the car.

Alyse moved quickly indoors as soon as the BMW drew out of sight. The house seemed to envelop her, so large and strangely silent, and she was unable to suppress a feeling of acute vulnerability.

Georg was sleeping peacefully, and she quickly showered before slipping into bed, where she lay wide-eyed and reflective as a dozen conflicting thoughts vied for supremacy in a brain too emotionally fraught to make sense of any one of them.

When she heard Aleksi return she closed her eyes in the pretence of sleep, aware of a deep ache in the region of her heart. It would have been wonderful to seek the comfort of his arms, to have them enfold her close, and simply hold her. A few tender kisses, the soothing touch of his hands, so that she felt secure in the knowledge that she was infinitely cherished.

Except that such an image belonged in the realm of fantasy, and she gave up waiting for him to join her in bed as the minutes dragged on. The only feasible explanation seemed to be a wealth of paperwork awaiting him in the study, and when she woke the following morning it was to discover he was already up and dressed.

In a way Alyse found it a relief to spend the following few days quietly at home. There were letters to write, and she rang Miriam Stanford at the Perth boutique to learn that everything was progressing extremely smoothly—almost as if she had hardly been missed, Alyse thought wryly.

During the afternoon she prepared their evening meal, taking infinite care with a carefully selected menu. Aleksi invariably arrived home just before five, and after a quick shower he would insist on changing and feeding Georg.

'He needs to recognise a male figure in his young life,' Aleksi had said the day after Rachel and Alexandros departed for Sydney. 'Besides, this is the only time I have to give to him five nights out of seven.'

It left Alyse free to set the table and make a last-minute check on dinner. Just watching the tiny baby in Aleksi's arms wrenched her emotions, for she could imagine Aleksi being an integral part of Georg's existence, playing ball, teaching him to swim, simply being there throughout his formative adolescent years. Each time the pull at her heartstrings became a little more painful, and she was gripped with a terrifying fear that although removing Georg to Perth was right for her, it wouldn't necessarily be right for Georg.

Conversation over dinner was restricted to their individual daily activities, polite divertissements that lasted until dessert had been consumed, then

Aleksi would invariably disappear into the study and not emerge until long after she had gone to bed.

The possibility that his actions might be deliberate angered her unbearably, and she found herself consciously plotting a subtle revenge.

The occasion of Solange and Dominic Rochas' dinner party seemed ideal, and on Friday morning Alyse rang Melanie and arranged for her to babysit Georg while she went shopping for something suitable to wear.

The desire to stun was uppermost, and she found exactly what she wanted in an exclusive boutique. In black, its bodice was strapless, exquisitely boned and patterned in black sequins, with a slim-fitting knee-length skirt that hugged her slender hips. A long floating silk scarf draped at her neck to flow down her back completed the outfit, and, ignoring the outrageously expensive price-tag, she simply charged it. Shoes came next, and she chose a perfume to match her new image.

As Saturday progressed it was impossible to quell her reservations, and after feeding and settling Georg into his cot she quickly showered, then settled down in front of the mirror with a variety of cosmetics.

It seemed to take an age to achieve the desired effect, but eventually she stood back, satisfied with the result. Her hair was brushed into its customary smooth bell-shape, and in a moment of indecision she caught its length and twisted it high into a knot on top of her head.

Yes? No? *'Damn,'* she muttered softly, beginning to view the evening ahead with a certain degree of dread.

Solange was someone with whom she doubted it was possible ever to share an empathy. Even on so short an acquaintance, it was impossible not to be aware that the interior decorator lusted after Aleksi, and the mere fact that Alyse was Aleksi's wife stacked the odds heavily against her from the start.

Her dynamic husband had a lot to answer for, she decided as she crossed to the large mirrored closet and slid back the door. Although to be fair, he couldn't help his dark good looks, nor his sexual appeal, for both were an inherent quality, and, while some men might deliberately exploit such assets, honesty forced her to concede that Aleksi did not.

A tiny frown of doubt momentarily creased her forehead as she extracted *the* dress from its hanger. Although it had been selected to shock, she suddenly developed reservations as to its suitability. Remembering precisely why she had purchased it deepened her frown, and her eyes clouded with indecision. What had seemed an excellent means of revenge at the time no longer held much appeal, and she was about to slip it back on to the hanger when she heard Aleksi move into the dressing-room.

'What time have you organised for Melanie to arrive?'

'Seven,' she answered, turning slightly towards him, watching as he discarded the towel knotted low at his hips, then he stepped into dark briefs and reached for a snowy white shirt.

His physique was splendid, emanating innate power and strength, and Alyse was unable to prevent the surge of sheer sexual pleasure at the sight of him.

Impossibly cross with herself, she slid down the zip fastener and stepped into the gown. Her fingers automatically slid the zip into place, then smoothed its sleek lines over her hips before settling on the gentle swell of her breasts, which were exposed to a greater degree than she remembered when originally trying on the gown.

'Did you select that with the intention of raising every red-blooded man's blood pressure at the party tonight, or simply mine?' Aleksi drawled from behind, and she slowly turned to face him.

'Why would I deliberately want to raise yours?' she queried sweetly.

'The result is stunning, but I may not be able to stand guard at your side every minute during the evening to fend off the attention you'll undoubtedly receive,' he warned with an edge of mockery, and her eyes acquired a fiery sparkle.

'Really? Are you suggesting I should change?' There was anger just beneath the surface, and a crazy desire to oppose him.

His expression darkened fractionally. 'Yes.'

'And if I choose not to?'

'The only choice you have, Alyse, is to remove the dress yourself or have me do it for you.' His voice was hard and inflexible, and her chin lifted in angry rejection, her eyes becoming stormy pools mirroring incredulous rage.

'Why, you chauvinistic domineering *pig*,' she re-iterated heatedly. 'How dare you?'

'Oh, I *dare*,' he drawled silkily, and a shiver slithered the length of her spine at his determined resolve.

'It's the latest fashion and cost a small fortune,' she flung angrily. 'And besides, I won't have you dictate what I can and can't wear!'

He reached out a hand and caught hold of her chin between thumb and forefinger, tightening his grasp when she moved to wrench it away. 'Stop arguing simply for the sake of it.'

'I'm *not*!' She was so incredibly furious, it was all she could do not to hit him.

'Surely you know me well enough by now to understand that you can't win,' he cautioned with deadly softness.

'You mean you won't allow me to!'

He was silent for a few seemingly long seconds, and she held his gaze fearlessly.

'A woman who deliberately flaunts her body indulges in subtle advertising of a kind which promises to deliver. Wear the dress when we're dining alone, and I'll be suitably appreciative.'

'Oh, for heavens's sake! I don't believe any of this!'

'Believe,' he said hardily. 'Now, change.'

'No.'

'Defiance, Alyse, simply for the sake of it? Aren't you being rather foolish?'

'If you derive a sadistic thrill from forcibly removing a woman's clothes, then go ahead and do it.'

His eyes assumed a chilling intensity, and she was suddenly filled with foreboding. Without a word his hands closed over her shoulders, propelling her forward, and her chin tilted in silent rebellion as he lowered his head.

His mouth took possession of hers, forcing her lips apart in a demanding assault that showed little mercy and she held back a silent groan of despair as he deliberately began a wreaking devastation.

When he relinquished his hold, her jaw ached, even her neck, and her eyes were bright with a mixture of anger and unshed tears.

His eyes bore an inscrutability she was unable to penetrate, and her mouth trembled slightly.

'Change, Alyse,' he directed inflexibly. 'Or I'll do it for you.'

She looked at him with scathing enmity. 'And if I refuse, you'll undoubtedly admininster some other form of diabolical punishment.'

'Take care,' he warned. 'My temper is on a tight rein as it is.'

'So I must conform, at whatever cost? That's almost akin to barbarism!'

An eyebrow lifted in sardonic cynicism. 'So far I've treated you with kid gloves.'

A disbelieving laugh emerged from her throat. 'You have to be joking!'

'Only an innocent would fail to appreciate the slow hand of a considerate lover intent on giving as much pleasure as he intends to take.' His expression became dark and forbidding. 'Continue opposing me, and I'll demonstrate the difference.'

Alyse looked at him with unblinking solemnity, frighteningly aware of his strength and sense of purpose. To continue waging this particular war was madness, yet some alien stubborn streak refused to allow her to capitulate.

'Don't threaten me,' she warned.

'Is that what you imagine I'm doing?' His voice held a hateful drawling quality that sent shivers of fear scudding down her spine.

'What other word would you choose?'

'Take off the dress, Alyse,' he warned softly, 'or I won't answer for the consequences.'

It was as if her limbs were frozen and entirely separate from the dictates of her brain, for she stood perfectly still, her eyes wide and unblinking as he swore softly beneath his breath.

Then she cried out as his fingers reached for the zip fastener and slid it down. Seconds later the exotic creation fell to her feet to lie in a heap of silk and heavy satin. All that remained between her and total nudity was a wisp of silky bikini briefs, and her hands rose in spontaneous reaction to cover her breasts.

With deliberate slowness Aleksi slid down the zip of his trousers, and it was only as he began to remove them that she became galvanised into action.

Except that it was far too late, and she struggled helplessly against him, hating the strength of the hands that moulded her slim curves against the hard muscular contours of his body. Her briefs were dispensed seconds after his own, and there was nothing she could do to avoid the relentless pressure of his mouth. He lifted her up against him, parting her thighs so they straddled his hips, and without any preliminaries he plunged deep inside, his powerful thrust stretching silken tissues to their furthest limitation.

Relinquishing her mouth, he lowered his head to her breast, and she cried out as he took possession of one roseate peak, savouring it with flagrant hunger before rendering several bites to the soft underside of the swollen peak.

Alyse balled her hands into fists and beat them against his shoulders then gave a startled cry of disbelief as his hands shifted down to grip her bottom, lifting her slightly as he plunged even deeper.

Then he stilled, and she felt him swell even further inside her, while the hand at her back slid to clasp her nape, urging her head back as he forced her to meet his gaze.

She wanted to vilify him for an act of savagery, yet among the outrage had been a degree of primitive enjoyment, and she hated herself almost as much as she hated him for it.

He knew; she glimpsed the knowledge in the depth of his eyes, and hated him even more for the faint mocking smile that curved his lips.

Hands that had been hard gentled as they cradled her, and he buried his mouth against the hollows at the base of her throat, teasing the rapidly beating pulse there with his tongue, then, just as she thought he was about to release her, he began a slow circling movement with his hips, taking her with him until, almost as a silent act of atonement, pleasure

overtook discomfort and her senses became caught
up with his, spiralling towards a mutual climax that
made her cling to him in unashamed abandon.

Afterwards she showered, then dressed in a vivid
emerald-green ruched satin gown with a demure
neckline and fitted lines that accentuated her petite
figure.

Keeping her make-up to an understated
minimum, she accented her eyes and outlined her
mouth in soft pink before checking on Georg.

Melanie had arrived and was comfortably settled
in the lounge when Alyse emerged several minutes
later, and she greeted the girl pleasantly, then accepted Aleksi's light clasp on her elbow as they took
their leave and made their way to the garage.

'I rang Solange and told her not to hold dinner
as we'd been unavoidably detained,' Aleksi told her
as the BMW cleared the driveway. 'I've made a res-
ervation at the Club's restaurant. We'll eat there.'

Alyse took a deep breath, then released it slowly.
'I'm not hungry.'

'You'll eat something, even if it's only *soupe du
jour*,' he declared with unruffled ease.

The fact that she did owed nothing to his in-
sistence, and seated opposite him in the well-
patronised room she did justice to soup, declined
a main course in favour of a second starter of
sautéed prawns, refused sweets and settled for a
Jamaican coffee.

It was almost ten when the BMW passed security
and slid into a reserved car space in the spacious
grounds adjoining a prestigious block of apart-

ments housing Solange and Dominic Rochas' penthouse apartment, and Alyse stood in meditative
silence as they rode the private lift to the uppermost floor.

CHAPTER TEN

'ALEKSI!' Solange purred, immediately embracing him in a manner that slipped over the edge from affection and bordered on blatant intimacy. She stepped back, her eyes shifting with glittering condescension to the woman at his side. 'Alyse.' She tucked a hand into the curve at Aleksi's elbow and drew him forward.

'Solange,' Alyse murmured in polite acknowledgment. 'How lovely to see you.'

Liar, a silent voice taunted. She felt about as well equipped to parry a verbal cut and thrust with the glamorous and very definitely bitchy Solange Rochas as flying over the moon! 'Charming' was the key-word, and she'd act her socks off—subtly, of course, with the innocuous innocence of an ingénue.

'Everyone is here,' Solange declared huskily. 'I was so disappointed you couldn't make dinner.'

'We were delayed,' drawled Aleksi, and Alyse merely proffered a sweet smile when Solange cast her a brief interrogatory glance.

Aleksi had sought to teach her a lesson, and it didn't bear thinking about the resultant passion that flared between them in the aftermath of anger.

'Unfortunately,' Alyse added with sweet regret, and almost died as Aleksi caught hold of her hand

and lifted it to his lips, deliberately kissing each finger in turn.

His eyes blazed with indefinable emotion for a brief few seconds, then became dark and faintly hooded as he threaded his fingers through her own and kept them there.

Liquid fire coursed through her veins, activating each separate nerve-ending as it centred deep within the vulnerable core of her femininity, and she ached, aware of bruised tissues still sensitive from his wounding invasion.

Almost as if he was aware of her thoughts his thumb brushed back and forth across the throbbing veins at her wrist, and her pulse leapt in recognition of his touch. If she hadn't retained such a vivid memory of his wrath, she could almost imagine the gesture was meant as a silent token of—what? Apology? Remorse?

'I'm sure you had a very good reason, darling,' Solange declared, her eyes narrowing with speculative interest as she drew them into the lounge. 'I'll get you a drink, then there's something we must discuss.' She gave a brittle laugh, then offered in throwaway explanation to Alyse, 'Business, I'm afraid.' Then she turned away, effectively shutting Alyse out. 'The Holmes residence. You absolutely *must* dissuade Anthea against the shade of pink she insists on having as the main theme. It really won't do at all.'

Alyse moved slightly, watching with detached fascination as Aleksi's mouth curved into a wry smile.

'If you're unable to exercise your professional influence, Solange, then you may have to accept that it's Anthea's house and she's paying the bills.'

'But it's *my* reputation.'

'Then relinquish the commission.'

The woman's eyes glittered as she made a moue of distaste. 'The problem with the nouveaux riches, darling,' she conceded, with a careless shrug, 'is their gauche taste.'

'Why not show her a visual example of one of your previous commissions?' ventured Alyse, thereby forcing Solange's attention. 'Magazine layouts and countless sample swatches can be confusing.'

Solange looked as if she had just been confronted with an unwanted dissident. 'Something that would be an impossible intrusion on a former client's privacy,' she dismissed with patronising hauteur.

'If I were really delighted with the décor of my home, I'd be only too pleased to share it,' Alyse qualified quietly.

At that precise moment Dominic came forward to greet them, and his deep smile was infinitely mocking.

'Ah, there you are,' he greeted, flicking his sister a brief questioning glance before acknowledging Aleksi, then his gaze settled on Alyse with musing indulgence. 'You look gorgeous, as always. What can I get you to drink?'

'Mineral water will be fine,' Alyse requested without guile, while Aleksi opted for soda with a splash of whisky.

Her glass was icy, its rim sugar-frosted, and she sipped the contents, silently applauding the dash of lime juice and twist of lemon.

'Aleksi,' a soft breathy voice intruded, and Alyse turned slightly and failed to recognise the owner of that husky feminine sound. The slight pause was deliberate, as was her deliberately sexy pout. 'Didn't the babysitter arrive on time?'

Alyse shifted slightly and summoned a brilliant smile. 'Aleksi is to blame. He didn't approve of what I'd chosen to wear, and...' She trailed to a halt, made an expressive shrug, then directed the man at her side a wicked smile. 'One thing led to another.'

The stunning brunette's scarlet-painted mouth parted slightly, then tightened into a thin, uncompromising line.

'How refreshingly honest, darling,' drawled Dominic, and his eyes gleamed devilishly. 'I presume it was worth missing dinner?'

'Really, Dominic,' Solange derided in a voice dripping with vitriol, 'must you be so crude?'

'My husband can be——' Alyse paused, deliberately effecting a carefully orchestrated smile, 'very persuasive.' There, let them make of it what they chose, and be damned! She was heartily sickened by the various snide comments, the none too subtle innuendo designed to shock or at least unsettle her. Timidity had no place in her demeanour if she were to succeed within Aleksi's sophisticated circle, and it would seem her only strength lay in presenting an imperturbable if faintly humorous exterior.

Aleksi's eyes narrowed faintly, but she really didn't care any more.

'I'm sure Dominic won't mind keeping me amused for a while if Solange would prefer you to confer with Anthea,' she said sweetly, and glimpsed Solange's smile of triumph.

'I'll speak to Anthea later,' Aleksi determined mildly, although there was nothing remotely mild about the warning pressure of the hand clasping her own. 'Shall we mingle?' he queried pleasantly. 'We can't monopolise our hosts' attention.'

Solange's expression clearly revealed that he, at least, could monopolise her attention any time he chose, and Alyse had little choice but to drift at Aleksi's side as he drew her among the glittering guests.

The penthouse apartment provided a brilliant advertisement for Solange and Dominic's interior decorating expertise. Perfection personified, Alyse thought, with the smallest detail adhered to from the exquisite floral arrangements to the attire of the hired staff. Even the music had been deliberately selected to blend with conversation rather than provide a cacophonous intrusion.

'Aren't you being a little careless?' Aleksi queried with deceptive calm as they paused near the edge of the room, and Alyse idly twirled the contents of her glass.

'Another guessing game, Aleksi?' she countered, deliberately meeting his gaze.

'I find it particularly unamusing to have my wife offer provocative comments to a known society playboy.'

'Dominic?' Her eyes widened measurably, then became startlingly direct. 'Really? When almost every woman in the room homes in on your presence like a prize bitch in heat?'

'Aren't you being overly dramatic?'

'No,' she said simply, and had to force herself to stand perfectly still as he lifted a hand and brushed his fingers across her cheek.

'Does it bother you?'

Yes, she wanted to cry out. It bothers me like hell. Yet if she acknowledged how she felt it would amount to an admission of sorts, and she wasn't ready to accord him any advantage. Instead, she held his gaze and returned evenly, 'Why should it?'

Something flared in his eyes, an infinitesimal flame that was quickly masked. 'We can always leave.'

Her surprise was undisguised. 'We've only just arrived.'

'Do you want to stay?'

What a loaded question! Whichever way she answered would be equally damning and, although she didn't particularly want to remain, she wasn't ready to go home.

'Aleksi! I'm so glad you're here.'

The intrusion was welcome, and Alyse glanced with interest towards the petite blonde hovering nearby as Aleksi effected an introduction.

'Anthea Holmes, my wife Alyse.'

'How nice to meet you,' she acknowledged with gracious charm before turning towards Aleksi. 'I'm almost at my wits' end!' Her pretty hazel eyes darkened with anxiety. 'The house is superb, but I can't help wondering when I'll be able to move in.'

'Solange mentioned a conflict of interest over the colour scheme,' Aleksi acknowledged. 'What seems to be the problem?'

'A shade of pink,' Anthea said at once. 'I originally chose an extremely delicate salmon shade to blend with cream, and utilising various apricot tones as the main theme. Solange insists on shell-pink to blend with mushroom and various tones of amethyst.' She turned towards Alyse. 'What do you think?'

Oh lord, Alyse groaned inwardly. Why drag me into it? 'I wouldn't presume to infringe on Solange's territory,' she ventured diplomatically. 'But surely it's a personal choice?' Solange was bound to feel insulted if she discovered Anthea had solicited another opinion, especially *hers*, and, while the woman could never be her friend, she didn't particularly want her as an enemy.

'I'd appreciate your viewpoint.'

'Whose viewpoint, darling?'

Alyse almost groaned aloud, and was somewhat startled to see that Anthea was not in the least perturbed that Solange had overheard part of their conversation.

'I've invited Alyse to see the house.'

It was clearly evident that the cat had been well and truly placed among the pigeons, for Solange cast her a sharp narrowed glance. 'Well, of course, if you value the opinion of an unqualified outsider over and above my own...' She let her voice trail to a deliberate halt.

'Alyse is naturally interested in my work,' Aleksi inserted smoothly. 'Aware, also, that I consider my individual clients' wishes are paramount.' His dark eyes encompassed Solange's features in silent warning before switching to Anthea. 'I'll ring my painting contractor tomorrow, then confirm with you and have him meet us at the house.'

Anthea's relief was instantly evident. 'Thank you.' She touched Alyse's hand. 'I'll be mailing invitations to a housewarming party just as soon as I've settled in. You will both come, won't you?'

'We'd be delighted,' Aleksi responded warmly, and Anthea looked quite overcome.

'Another conquest, darling?' Solange asked archly the instant Anthea had melted into the crowd.

'Anthea is a very pleasant woman,' he acknowledged coolly. 'And a valued client of mine.' But not necessarily of yours.

The words remained unspoken, yet Alyse was supremely conscious of the veiled threat. Aware also that Solange sensed his displeasure, for her features underwent a startling transformation.

'A figurative rap across the knuckles, Aleksi?' Solange queried provocatively. 'Dear little Anthea can have her salmon pink and cream with apricot, if that's what she wants. Why, when she has such rigid ideas, she should consult with an interior designer is beyond me.' Her exquisitely manicured hands fluttered through the air. 'One mustn't forget the newly rich consider it quite the thing to gather opinions without the slightest intention of applying one of them.'

'Perhaps because they prefer to impose something of their own personality,' said Alyse, and drew a raised eyebrow in response.

'Really, darling,' Solange gave a faint shudder, 'I hope this doesn't mean you intend making too many changes in Aleksi's home. It's total perfection just as it is.'

'An incredible compliment,' a drawling voice intervened, 'considering you had no part in it.'

'Dominic. Eavesdropping again?'

Alyse's glass was whisked out of her hand before she had an opportunity to protest, and she made no demur when Dominic took hold of her elbow.

'Come and let me show you the view from the window,' Dominic insisted. 'It's really spectacular.'

It was; beyond the wide expanse of plate-glass tiny pinpricks of light outlined countless high-rise buildings along the foreshore curving in an arc towards the ocean. The sky was a crisp cool indigo, meeting and merging on the horizon with a moon-dappled darkened sea.

'It's beautiful,' Alyse said softly, caught up in the thrall of man-made monoliths of concrete steel and glass blending with the stark simplicity of nature.

'I can pay you the same compliment.'

She stood quite still at the degree of warmth in his voice. 'I shall accept that in the context in which it should be given,' she said lightly, and heard his purring laugh.

'I'm shattered,' he remarked musingly. 'I imagined you to be an innocent in paradise.'

'Innocence belongs to the very young.'

'Cynicism too,' he mocked. 'From one whose air of fragility is positively intriguing. A mystery woman-child with clear eyes and a beautiful smile. I hope Aleksi appreciates you.'

Of its own accord her smile deepened, and she laughed, a light bubbly sound filled with genuine amusement.

'No comment?'

'May I choose not to?' Alyse countered, and her eyes flew wide as he took hold of her hand.

'Old-fashioned values?'

'I consider a respect for one's privacy is merely good manners,' she corrected solemnly, and saw his eyes lose their customary jaded expression in favour of what appeared to be genuine warmth.

'What a pity Aleksi saw you first.'

Even if he hadn't, she couldn't imagine herself being smitten by Dominic's superficial charm. Whereas Aleksi possessed depth and strength of character, the man at her side bore a shallow brittleness that was undoubtedly motivated by self-obsession.

She turned slightly, unconsciously seeking a familiar dark head across the crowded room, and her eyes widened as they encountered Aleksi's riveting gaze. He was engaged in conversation with a group of men she had met but vaguely remembered, and it was almost as if he knew she had conducted a mental comparison, for she saw one eyebrow lift in silent query.

For one crazy moment she felt as if everything faded away and there was no one else in the room. It was totally mad, but she wanted to be with him.

Not only by his side, but in his arms, held close, and loved with such incredible tenderness that she would probably cry from the sheer joy of it.

Her eyes widened and assumed an ethereal mistiness for an incredibly brief second, then she offered a slightly shaky smile and turned back towards Dominic, feeling completely disorientated as she launched into a conversational discourse that was unrelated to anything of particular interest.

It must have made sense, she thought vaguely, for Dominic responded with a flow of words she barely registered, let alone absorbed, and she gave a mental shake as if to clear her head.

What on earth was the matter with her?

'Dominic—you won't mind if I rescue my wife?'

Alyse heard Aleksi's deep drawling voice an instant before his arm curved round her waist, and she felt all her fine body hairs lift up in silent recognition of his presence.

'I assure you she isn't in the slightest danger.'

Never from Dominic. Aleksi, however, was an entirely different matter!

'Shall we leave?' Aleksi queried, bending his head down to hers, and she shrugged.

'If you like.'

'It's barely midnight!' protested Dominic, and Aleksi responded smoothly,

'We said before we left that we wouldn't be late.'

'But surely you can ring the babysitter?'

'I think not.'

In the car Alyse sat in silence, grateful for the light music emitting from stereo speakers, and she simply let her head fall back against the seat's headrest as the BMW purred through the darkened streets.

On reaching home Melanie reported that Georg hadn't even stirred, and Alyse checked his sleeping form while Aleksi saw the young girl into her car and then locked up.

Slipping out of her shoes, Alyse stepped through to the en suite bathroom and set about removing her make-up. Her features looked pale, and her eyes seemed much too large, she decided broodingly. Even her mouth bore a faintly bruised fullness, and she ran the tip of her tongue along the edge of her lower lip in unconscious exploration before lifting the brush to her hair.

She had only just begun when Aleksi entered the bathroom, and her hand faltered slightly as he moved close and took the brush from her nerveless fingers.

She knew she should protest, but no words left her lips, and she stood still beneath his touch, held as if enmeshed in some elusive sensual spell.

The temptation to close her eyes was irresistible, and when the brush strokes ceased she let her lashes flicker up as she met his gaze via mirrored reflection.

His hands moved to the zip fastening of her dress, and she made no effort to prevent its slithering folds slipping down to the floor, nor the thin scrap of satin and lace of her bra as he released the clasp.

Fingers traced the length of her spine, then spanned her waist before slipping up to cup her breasts. His breath fanned her nape, and she let her head fall forward in silent invitation, unable to suppress a shiver of sheer reaction as his lips sought a vulnerable pulsebeat and savoured it until tiny shockwaves of pleasure spiralled from deep within her central core.

It was almost as if he wanted her to see the effect of his touch on her body, and she moved back against him, arching slightly as his fingers teased the soft fullness of her breasts, then shaped them as the peaks tautened and became engorged with anticipatory pleasure. With detached fascination she glimpsed the soft smudges where hours earlier his mouth had wrought havoc as he had sought to punish, and her eyes clouded in remembered pain.

Hands slid to her shoulders and turned her round to face him, and she was powerless against the caressing softness of his lips as they brushed each bruise in turn before trailing up to settle on her trembling mouth.

His touch was an evocative supplication, teasing, tasting, *loving* in a manner that made her want to cry, and when he slid an arm beneath her knees and lifted her into his arms she could only bury her face against the hollow of his neck.

In bed she closed her eyes, grateful for the darkness as he led her with infinite slowness towards the sweet oblivion of sexual fulfilment, and she clung to him unashamedly, adrift in a sea of her own emotions.

A week ago, even yesterday, she had been so positive her planned escape to Perth was what she desperately wanted. Now, the thought of walking away from Aleksi caused doubt and indecision, and for the first time she was filled with despair.

If she stayed, it would have to be for all the right reasons, and she doubted if love formed any part of his rationale. The most she could hope for would be an affectionate loyalty, a bond founded by Georg's existence. Somehow it wasn't enough.

For what seemed like an hour Alyse lay awake staring at the shadowed ceiling, a hundred differing emotions clouding her mind in kaleidoscopic confusion.

Nothing was the same; *nothing*, Alyse decided sadly as she slid carefully out of bed, each movement in seeming slow motion so as not to disturb the man sleeping silently at her side.

How could she leave? Yet how could she stay? a tiny voice taunted as she crossed to the sitting-room and paused in front of Georg's cot. He was so dear, *everything*, she decided fiercely, unable to prevent her eyes misting with unshed tears.

Moonlight streamed through the opaque curtains, creating an area of shade and silvery light, while long shadowy fingers magnified everything beyond. The balustrading surrounding the pool resembled a grotesque caricature of angles that were unrelated to its original structure, and the pool itself appeared a deep, dark void.

Like her heart. Dear lord in heaven, was it too much to expect happiness? Was she being a fool to even hope it could be achieved?

She had no idea how long she stood there, and it was acute sensory perception rather than an actual sound that alerted her to Aleksi's presence.

'What are you doing here?' His voice was deep and husky, and she was unable to prevent the shiver that shook her slim frame.

Hands caught her shoulders in a light clasp, then slid down her arms, slipping beneath her elbows to curve round her waist as he pulled her gently back against him.

'You'll catch a chill,' he chided softly, burying his lips against the vulnerable hollow at the edge of her neck.

I am cold, so cold there should be ice instead of blood in my veins. As long as I live, I'll never be warm again.

'Come back to bed.'

No! a silent voice screamed out in silent agony. That was her downfall, the place where she fought countless battles and inevitably lost. Her eyes began to ache with barely suppressed tears, and her vision shimmered as two huge crystalline drops hovered, momentarily dammed by protective lower lashes.

'Alyse?'

Hands gently turned her towards him, and she was powerless to evade the strong fingers that took hold of her chin and tilted it upwards.

The movement released her tears, and there was nothing she could do to prevent their slow trickling descent.

It was impossible that they might escape his attention; too much to hope for that he might choose not to comment on their existence.

She looked at him, her head caught at a proud angle, its planes sharply defined, yet his profile was indistinct viewed through a watery mist that failed to dissipate no matter how often she blinked.

I'm caught in a trap, she thought, feeling incredibly sad. Bound within a silken web whose strands hold me prisoner as surely as if they were comprised of tensile steel.

'Tears?'

Amusement was sadly lacking, and in its place was a depth she was almost afraid to analyse.

A finger traced one rivulet, then followed the path of its twin. 'Why?'

For all the dreams, the love I have to give; hope, eternity.

'Alyse?'

His voice was as soft as velvet, his breath warm as it fanned her cheek, and she closed her eyes against the featherlight touch of his lips at her temples, on her eyelids, then finally her mouth.

It was seduction at its most dangerous, and she almost succumbed as he lifted her into his arms and carried her back into the bedroom. The only thing that stopped her was the degree of treachery involved; sexual pleasure without emotional commitment was no longer enough, and she couldn't pretend any more.

Gently he let her slide down to her feet.

'Suppose you tell me what's bothering you?'

Where could she begin? By saying she'd fallen in love with him? A slight tremor shook her thinly clad form at the thought of his cynicism on learning that she had joined a number of women who had fallen prey to his fatal brand of sexual sensuality.

'I'm almost afraid to insist.' There was an indefinable quality in his voice, a rawness that sent her lashes sweeping upward in swift disbelief.

Alyse was aware of him watching every visible flicker of emotion, and she forced herself to breathe steadily to deploy the deep thudding beat of her heart.

'Please,' Aleksi demanded gently, letting his hands slide up to cup her face.

Something she dared not begin to believe might be hope stirred deep within. 'I don't think I can.'

His lips touched hers with the lightness of a butterfly's wing. 'Try.'

Dared she? No matter how she voiced it, the words would sound calculatingly cold, and afterwards there could be no retraction, only expiation when mere explanation might not be enough.

'Georg deserves to have you as his father,' she faltered at last, unsure whether she had the courage to continue, and something she could have sworn was pain darkened his eyes.

There was a strained silence, then Aleksi drawled with dangerous silkiness, 'You don't consider Georg deserves to have you as his mother?'

Alyse felt as if she was treading on eggshells, yet now she'd started there was nothing else for her but to go on. 'I love him,' she burst out. 'How can you doubt that?'

'Your love for *him* isn't in question.'

The breath caught in her throat, then escaped in a ragged expulsion as her features paled, and she actually swayed, fearing she might fall. Somehow the thought that Aleksi might know the extent of her emotions made her feel physically ill. She had to get away from him, if only temporarily. 'Please—let me go,' she begged.

'Never.'

There was an inflexibility apparent that made her feel terribly afraid.

'I think you'll reconsider when you realise the only reason I entered into marriage was the prospect of obtaining a divorce and legal custody of Georg,' she began shakily, glimpsing a muscle tense along the edge of his jaw as she fought for the strength to continue. 'Almost right from the beginning I plotted the ultimate revenge,' she continued unsteadily, struggling to find the right words, aware that now she'd started, she couldn't stop. 'Two years, that's all I figured it would take before I could return with Georg to Perth.'

His silence was enervating, and after what seemed an interminable length of time she willed him to say something—anything.

'And now?'

'What would you have me say?' she queried in anguish.

'Try—honesty.'

She was weeping inside, drenched by her own silent tears. 'So you can have *your* revenge, Aleksi?'

'Is that what you think?'

'Oh, why do you have to answer every question with another?' she beseeched, sorely tried.

'Because I want it all.'

It was too soon to bare her soul. Much too soon. Love was supposed to happen gradually, not all at once. How was it possible to know if it *was* love in only a matter of weeks?

'I *can't*,' she denied in a tortured whisper.

Aleksi was silent for so long she felt almost afraid, then when he spoke his voice was edged with quiet determination.

'As soon as Rachel and Alexandros return to the Coast, we'll fly to Athens.'

A startled gasp left her lips, and he pressed a finger against them to still the words in protest.

'My parents will delight in having Georg to themselves for a while.'

'Do you always arrange things on the spur of the moment?' she questioned weakly, unable to argue.

'Are you saying you don't want to go?'

She stood hesitantly unsure for a few timeless seconds. 'No,' she whispered at last, aware with frightening certainty that her fate had been irreversibly sealed.

CHAPTER ELEVEN

THE days that followed assumed a dreamlike quality. There was a gentleness apparent, a sense of almost secret anticipation that was fuelled by the touch of the hand, the exquisiteness of their lovemaking.

They accepted few invitations, although when they did venture out Alyse was conscious of the overt, barely concealed glances, the thinly disguised speculative gossip as Aleksi rarely let her out of his sight. At home she took delight in arranging gourmet dinners, with candlelight and wine, loving the long, leisurely conversation shared as they talked about anything and everything.

Two days after Rachel and Alexandros arrived back from Sydney Alyse and Aleksi flew out to Athens, spending two days in that ancient city before chartering a helicopter to a small remote island set like a shimmering jewel in the midst of a translucent emerald sea.

There were grapevines, orange trees, olive groves, a few goats, a dog, all lovingly tended by an elderly couple who greeted Aleksi fondly before boarding the waiting helicopter that would take them to visit relatives on another island.

'It's beautiful,' Alyse breathed as Aleksi led her towards an old, concrete-plastered, whitewashed house set on high ground.

Built around an inner courtyard, the rooms were large and airy and filled with antique furniture. Rich Persian rugs covered highly polished floors, and there were several soft-cushioned sofas in the lounge.

'As a child, I spent most of my holidays here,' Aleksi revealed.

'Did you ever return to the island after you emigrated to Australia?' Alyse asked, wandering around the large lounge at will, pausing slightly now and then to study one of the several framed family photographs resting atop items of furniture.

'Several times.'

She turned to look at him, seeing the inherent strength apparent, the sheer physical attraction, and a shadow fleetingly darkened her eyes at the number of women who had surely formed part of his life.

'To join Rachel and Alexandros, and Georgiou,' he added softly. 'This island has always been a family retreat.'

She summoned a bright smile that hid a slight degree of pain. 'It's so warm. Shall we swim before dinner?'

He was silent for a brief second, then he crossed to where she stood and caught hold of her hand. 'Why not?'

The water was crystal-clear and deliciously cool. Alyse challenged Aleksi to a race across the width of the tiny bay, and he merely gave a tigerish laugh as he deliberately let her win. In retaliation she scooped up handfuls of water and threw them at his chest, then shrieked when he pulled her into his arms.

For a moment she struggled, caught up in a playful game, then she slowly stilled, her expression hesitantly serious.

There were so many things she wanted to say, words she needed to hear, yet she was strangely afraid to begin.

A faint edge of tension was evident beneath the surface of Aleksi's control, and she looked at him in silence, her eyes wide and unblinking.

Remembering his lovemaking, the tenderness, the passion . . . She was tired of fighting, and stubborn pride no longer seemed to matter any more.

'Please help me,' she implored in a husky whisper.

He lifted a hand to her lips and traced a finger across the generous lower curve. 'Why not start at the beginning?'

Her mouth quivered uncontrollably, and she hesitated, unsure now that she had instigated the moment of truth if she possessed the courage to continue. It would be terrible if he was merely amused by a confession of her emotions. Impossible, if he didn't return them to quite the same degree.

'You were everything I disliked in a man,' she ventured unsteadily, her eyes silently beseeching him to understand. 'Overbearing, demanding, and far too self-assured. I told myself I hated you, and at first I did. Then I began to hate myself for being caught up in the maelstrom of physical sensation you were able to arouse.' She drew a deep breath and released it shakily. 'I didn't want to *feel* like that, and I had to fight very hard not to fall in love with you.' A soft, tremulous smile parted her lips. 'It wasn't a very successful battle, for I lost miserably.'

The tension left him in one long shuddering sigh as he gathered her close, then his mouth possessed hers, gently and with such an incredibly sweet hunger she thought she might actually die from sheer sensation, and when at last he lifted his head she could only stand in silent bemusement.

'Repeat those last few words again,' he commanded quietly.

Her beautiful blue eyes misted, and her lips trembled fractionally as she whispered, 'I love you.'

'I had begun to despair that you'd ever admit it,' Aleksi said huskily as he bent low to bestow a lingering kiss to her mouth, then he caught her close, holding her as if he never intended to let her go.

'Can't you feel what you do to me?' His smile held a certain wryness he made no attempt to hide. 'I travelled to Perth with one plan firmly in mind,' he revealed slowly. 'To get Georg at whatever cost. Yet there you were; so fiercely protective of the baby I'd vowed to adopt as my son, adamantly refusing to give him up when I was so sure you would be only too eager to hand over responsibility and get on with your own life.' He brushed his lips across her cheek, then pressed each eyelid closed in turn before trailing a slow evocative path down to the edge of her mouth. 'There was no woman of my acquaintance that I could envisage assuming a motherly role to an orphan child, and faced with your blatant animosity it seemed almost poetic justice to take you as my wife and tame your splendid pride. What I didn't bargain for was the involvement of my emotions.' His smile held such incredible warmth, she felt treacherously weak. 'You were a pocket spitfire, opposing me at every turn. Yet you were so angelic with Rachel and my father, charming to my friends, and I found myself deliberately using every ploy I could engineer in an attempt to break down your defences.'

He paused, taking time to bestow a long, lingering kiss that melted her very bones. His arms held her close, yet she stood strangely still, waiting, wanting so desperately for him to say the words she longed to hear.

'There were times when I was tempted to kill you for being so blind. I love you. *Love*,' he reassured her with a gentle shake.

Joy unfurled itself and spread with tumultuous speed through her veins, and she reached up to lock her hands behind his neck, pulling his head down to hers as she initiated a kiss so incredibly sweet it took only seconds before he deepened it with passionate intensity.

When at last he lifted his head, she could only press her cheek into the curve of his shoulder as he slid an arm beneath her knees and lifted her high against his chest.

'Where are you taking me?' she whispered.

'Indoors.' Aleksi's eyes were warm. 'To bed.'

A soft laugh bubbled from her throat as he carried her into the bedroom, and her eyes sparkled with witching promise as he let her slide down to stand on her feet.

Unable to resist teasing him a little, she protested softly, 'I'm not in the least tired.' Linking her hands together at his nape, she reached up and touched her lips against the corner of his mouth.

He lifted a hand and brushed a stray tendril of hair back behind her ear with incredible gentleness. His smile was warm and infinitely seductive, and she stood looking at him, seeing the strength of purpose etched on those dark arresting features, the passion evident in the depth of his eyes.

A slight tremor shook her slender frame as she reached out and slowly removed his briefs, then her own before unfastening the clip of her bikini bra. Collecting a towel, she carefully blotted every trace of sea-water from his body, then she stood still as he took the towel from her hand and gently returned the favour before letting the towel fall to the floor.

Without a word she reached up and pulled his head down to hers, and her lips brushed across his own, trembling a little as she instigated a hesitant exploration, then she drew him towards the bed and pulled him down beside her.

'Please make love to me.' The plea left her lips as scarcely more than a whisper, and her mouth parted in welcome to his as he wrought a devastating assault on her senses, plundering until she clung to him unashamedly.

It seemed an age before he broke the kiss, and she almost died at the wealth of deep slumbrous passion evident.

'I intend to,' he told her gently. 'For the rest of my life.'

Next month's Romances

Each month, you can choose from a world of variety in romance with Mills & Boon. These are the new titles to look out for next month.

NO PLACE TOO FAR Robyn Donald

SECOND TIME LOVING Penny Jordan

IRRESISTIBLE ENEMY Lilian Peake

BROKEN DESTINY Sally Wentworth

PAST SECRETS Joanna Mansell

SEED OF VENGEANCE Elizabeth Power

THE TOUCH OF LOVE Vanessa Grant

AN INCONVENIENT MARRIAGE Diana Hamilton

BY DREAMS BETRAYED Sandra Marton

THAT MIDAS MAN Valerie Parv

DESERT INTERLUDE Mons Daveson

LOVE TAKES OVER Lee Stafford

THE JEWELS OF HELEN Jane Donnelly

PROMISE ME TOMORROW Leigh Michaels

The door to her past awaited – dare she unlock its secrets?

AVAILABLE IN FEBRUARY. PRICE £3.50

Adopted at sixteen, Julie Malone had no memory of her childhood. Now she discovers that her real identity is Suellen Deveraux – heiress to an enormous family fortune.

She stood to inherit millions, but there were too many unanswered questions – why couldn't she remember her life as Suellen? What had happened to make her flee her home?

As the pieces of the puzzle begin to fall into place, the accidents begin. Strange, eerie events, each more terrifying than the last. Someone is watching and waiting. Someone wants Suellen to disappear forever.

W❖RLDWIDE

A
SPECIAL GIFT
FOR
MOTHER'S DAY

Four new Romances by some of your favourite authors
have been selected as a special treat for Mother's Day.

**A CIVILISED
ARRANGEMENT**
Catherine George
THE GEMINI BRIDE
Sally Heywood
**AN IMPOSSIBLE
SITUATION**
Margaret Mayo
LIGHTNING'S LADY
Valerie Parv
Four charming love stories for
only £5.80, the perfect gift for
Mother's Day . . . or you can
even treat yourself.

**Look out for the special pack
from January 1991.**

Accept 4 Free Romances and 2 Free gifts

• FROM MILLS & BOON •

An irresistible invitation from Mills & Boon Reader Service. Please accept our offer of 4 free romances, a CUDDLY TEDDY and a special MYSTERY GIFT... Then, if you choose, go on to enjoy 6 more exciting Romances every month for just £1.45 each postage and packaging free. Plus our FREE newsletter with author news, competitions and much more.

Send the coupon below at once to: Reader Service, FREEPOST, P.O. Box 236, Croydon, Surrey CR9 9EL

〉— — — — — — ⎡ **NO STAMP NEEDED** ⎤— — — —

YES! Please rush me my 4 Free Romances and 2 FREE Gifts! Please also reserve me a Reader Service Subscription so I can look forward to receiving 6 Brand New Romances each month for just £8.70, post and packing free. If I choose not to subscribe I shall write to you within 10 days. I understand I can keep the free books and gifts whatever I decide. I can cancel or suspend my subscription at any time. I am over 18 years of age.

Name Mr/Mrs/Miss _____ EP86R

Address _____

_____

_____ Postcode _____

Signature _____